Layla's gaze connected with his.

Something zipped between them. Powerful and strong, his heart pounded even faster.

Shane inhaled a lungful of air and blew it out slowly as he tried to steady his erratic breathing. Why was he allowing her to affect him this way? Like Levi had said yesterday, she hadn't given him the time of day back then and nothing had changed as far as he could see.

It's nice to see you again. Her words flashed into his mind and the genuine smile on her face...

There went his wild heart again.

Shane banished the what-ifs banging around in his head. He'd already learned the hard way, girls like her brought nothing but heartache.

Dear Reader,

What happens when the new restaurant you've dreamed of owning since you were a child is about to go belly-up and the only person who can help you turn things around, before the bank forecloses on you, is the sinfully sexy, devilishly handsome guy who wants nothing to do with you? Sparks will fly...

Thank you for picking up this copy of *A Taste of Home*, book one in my Sisterhood of Chocolate & Wine series! For those who don't know me, I'm Anna James. I write contemporary romance, and although I've been writing for years, this is my first book with Harlequin. I hope you enjoy *A Taste of Home* as much as I enjoyed writing it. I'd love to hear what you think of Shane and Layla's story. Please share your thoughts with me on Facebook (annajames.author) and Twitter (@authorannajames) or drop me a line through my website, authorannajames.com.

Happy reading,

Anna James

A Taste of Home

ANNA JAMES

HARLEQUIN
SPECIAL
EDITION

HARLEQUIN®
SPECIAL EDITION™

Recycling programs
for this product may
not exist in your area.

ISBN-13: 978-1-335-72472-4

A Taste of Home

Copyright © 2023 by Heidi Tanca

For questions and comments about the quality of this book, please contact us at CustomerService@Harlequin.com.

Harlequin Enterprises ULC
22 Adelaide St. West, 41st Floor
Toronto, Ontario M5H 4E3, Canada
www.Harlequin.com

Printed in U.S.A.

Anna James writes contemporary romance novels with strong, confident heroes and heroines who conquer life's trials and find their happily-ever-afters.

Want to learn more about Anna and her books?

Sign up for her newsletter: authorannajames.com.

Follow her on Instagram: @author_anna_james.

Books by Anna James

Harlequin Special Edition

Sisterhood of Chocolate & Wine

A Taste of Home

Visit the Author Profile page at Harlequin.com.

For Latoya, my "Bookies" and my family—
this book wouldn't exist without your love and support.

Thank you, from the bottom of my heart.

Anna

Chapter One

New Suffolk, Massachusetts

Layla pushed the swinging door that led to La Cabane de La Mer's kitchen and stepped inside. The sounds of simmering pots and sizzling grills filled the air. She smiled and sucked in a deep satisfying breath.

She moved to the first prep station. A petite young blonde with a pixie haircut stood bent over the metal counter chopping potatoes. "Hi, Lucie." Her *chef de partie* was the only kitchen staff who had agreed to stay on when Layla had purchased her grandfather's restaurant nine months ago, after he and Nonny retired to Florida. She'd needed to hire three line cooks to replace those on her grandfather's staff who'd thought her crazy when she'd announced she'd turn his place into an upscale French bistro. So what if New Suffolk wasn't Paris? She'd make it work.

Antoine's smug image floated into her brain. *Lying, cheating bastard.* He thought she couldn't make it without him? *Hah!* She might not have her three Michelin stars yet, but she would. She'd turned his restaurant into one of the top places in Paris. She'd do the same here.

"Would you like to taste the lyonnaise potatoes?"

She gave herself a mental shake and concentrated on the task at hand. "Yes, please." Layla scooped up a thin slice covered with caramelized onion with her disposable tasting fork. She inserted it into her mouth. The potatoes were cooked to the correct consistency. Not too soft, not too crunchy. "Perfect."

Pitching the fork in the trash as she passed by, she wandered to the next prep table. "Hi, Luis."

Her *poissonnier* mumbled something she couldn't make out as he presented tonight's special.

Layla swallowed to clear her dry throat. Had she made the wrong decision in hiring Luis? She would have preferred to hire another female prep cook to replace Gabrielle when she'd moved away last month, but with his impeccable references, Luis had been the most qualified candidate who'd applied for the position.

Yes, he could be gruff at times, and a bit temperamental. Still, it wasn't like he wouldn't take direction from her.

Not like Pierre.

Her blood boiled every time she thought about how her ex, Antoine, had insisted she hire the arrogant sous-chef, and refused to allow her to fire his condescending ass when he kept going over her head every time he disagreed with her.

Stop it. Not all male cooks had a problem working for a woman. After all, Luis couldn't be a better fish cook. He really got her menu, and everyone on the team liked him. She shouldn't look for trouble where none existed.

Grabbing another disposable fork from her pocket, she scooped up a bite. "The sole meunière is delicious."

She gave a satisfied nod and turned her attention to her sous-chef. "You're in charge of the kitchen, Olivia. I'll be in my office if anyone needs me." She needed to meet with Zara to review the restaurant finances. Her sister had insisted they discuss some supplier invoice matters now that couldn't wait until their scheduled meeting in three days.

Layla exited the kitchen and strode down the hall to her office. She opened her laptop and logged into the reoccurring Zoom meeting. Her sister's face appeared on screen. "Hey, Zara. How are things in Manhattan?"

Thank goodness Zara had agreed to stay on as well after she'd purchased the restaurant. With five years' experience managing Gramps's place, her knowledge was invaluable.

"How are you feeling?" They'd skipped last week's review because Zara had come down with a stomach bug. This was the second time in as many months Zara had caught a nasty virus that had left her bedridden.

Layla scrutinized her sister's image. Truth be told,

she didn't appear one hundred percent recovered. Not if her washed-out pallor was anything to go by.

"Let's get started." Zara's weary expression tore at Layla's heart.

"You know, we can reschedule if you're still not well."

Zara didn't respond. Instead she shared her screen and pulled up a QuickBooks entry. "Here's the information from last week."

Layla scanned the invoices sitting on her desk and compared them to the entries in Zara's file. "I don't see the butcher payment. Can you go to the next page, please? Maybe it's just in the wrong place."

The color drained from Zara's face. She looked as if she might get sick.

Layla sucked in a quick breath, concern overtaking her irritation—after all, she'd stepped away from dinner service for this meeting! But her sister's well-being had to come first. "Okay. Enough is enough. You need to go back to bed and get over whatever bug you've got. We'll finish this when you're feeling better."

Zara dragged a hand through her long brown hair. "Layla, I—"

"Don't argue, Zara. Just get some rest and feel better soon." Layla waved and ended the call.

She sighed and added the two remaining invoices to the pile in the corner of her desk along with a sticky note reminding her to confirm the payments when she and Zara met next.

Damn. Zara had never voiced her concerns. She couldn't imagine what Zara might want to discuss when the invoices appeared to be in order. Hopefully, she'd be feeling better soon and they could talk about whatever was on her mind.

Shrugging, Layla rose from her chair and exited her office, walking the opposite way down the long hall. She stepped into the conservatory of the colonial mansion, now a spacious dining room, with to-die-for views of the Atlantic Ocean.

Three couples sat at intimate tables for two. She glanced at her watch. Seven at night. She would have expected more people on a Friday evening. No matter. Layla straightened her whites and readjusted the toque atop her head. Smiling, she approached the first table. It was time to meet and greet.

"Frank, Kim. It's so nice to see you." She wouldn't have expected the Bay Beach Club members—New Suffolk's version of a country club that catered to the affluent visitors who summered in the little beach town—to be in town at this time of year.

"Layla." Kim smiled. "We just had to stop in while we're in town for a little getaway from the city. We so enjoyed coming here last season."

"Yes," Frank agreed. "My coq au vin was delicious." He pointed to his empty plate.

"And you have one of Frank's favorite wines." Kim pointed to the almost empty bottle of Louis Jadot Echezeaux Grand Cru.

"You're on par with some of the finest bistros in Paris," Frank added.

A rush of pride flooded her chest. "Thank you. I'm

glad you enjoyed your meals. Enjoy the rest of your weekend."

"We will. We'll be back again before we head back to the city," Kim said.

Layla wanted to pump her fists in the air and do her happy dance. She wouldn't, of course. Instead, she pinned a polite smile in place and gave a nod of her head. "I look forward to seeing you."

Layla moved to a couple seated by the window. "Good evening. I'm the executive chef, Layla Williams. Thank you for dining with us tonight."

"Hello. I'm Winnie and this is my husband, Tom."

"Is this your first visit to La Cabane de La Mer?" She didn't recognize the fiftysomething-year-old couple.

"Yes," Tom said.

"My clients at the Mermaid talked about this place all last summer, so we thought we'd try out your place," Winnie added.

The spa at the beach club. "A fellow New Suffolk business owner. I'm glad you came for dinner tonight." Layla made a mental note to return the favor once the club opened for the season. "How were your meals?"

Tom opened his mouth to speak, but his wife cut him off.

"Excellent, but a bit pricey for beef stew if you ask me. The diner down the street serves a similar dish for a lot less."

Layla shuddered, but her smile never faltered. Of course her elegant boeuf bourguignon was more expensive. Her dish couldn't compare to something served in the local greasy spoon. And probably labeled "pot roast" to boot, she thought.

"Now, darling." The man reached across the table and patted his wife's hand. "It's our anniversary. This is a special occasion. You don't need to worry about the cost tonight."

"Happy anniversary." She gave a discreet wave and motioned for the server to come to the table. "Please enjoy dessert and a glass of champagne, on the house." She always treated customers when they came in for special occasions. It was just good business.

"Thank you." Winnie's eyes lit up with excitement.

"You're welcome. Enjoy the rest of your evening." Layla moved on to the next table, but she couldn't banish Winnie's remarks from her mind.

After speaking with the last couple, she returned to the kitchen, nodded to the line cooks and walked into the back room to take inventory for the next day's menu. She scrubbed her hands over her face. What was wrong with her tonight?

There's nothing wrong. She gave herself a mental shake and yanked open the cooler with more force than she'd planned. The door ricocheted off the outside wall and came flying toward her. She jumped out of the way to avoid being hit.

Layla stepped inside the cooler. She'd already cured the duck legs for the cassoulet. At least no one would compare that traditional dish to anything made in the local diner.

Stop it. The diners tonight had liked her food. No,

they'd *loved* her dishes. So, why complain about the cost? This town needed an upscale restaurant. Right?

They could patronize Gino's. It might not be in New Suffolk, but it was only five miles from here. Her shoulders sagged. The Italian food was superb and the prices... *Even better. Enough.* She needed to stop this madness. People liked La Cabane de La Mer. She was proud of what she'd built over the last nine months. With a little more time her place would be even more successful.

Layla double-checked the rest of the ingredients she'd need and exited the cooler.

Emily walked in as Layla returned to the kitchen. She grabbed a salad from the cooler.

"How's it going out there?" Layla asked. "Any more customers come in in the last hour?"

Emily nodded. "Table three would like to speak with you." She let out a little chuckle.

Layla arched a brow. "What's so funny?"

"It's Mrs. Clement."

Oh, Lord. The elderly woman who always tried to fix her up with her nephew every time she came in. "No problem. I'll go and speak with her now." She'd politely decline to meet Mr. Wonderful—this according to his besotted aunt—just like she'd done all the times before. She wasn't interested in a relationship. Not with Mrs. Clement's nephew. Not with any man.

Her hands clenched into tight fists. She wouldn't allow any man to make a fool of her ever again.

Layla would focus her energy on what mattered most—her restaurant.

She straightened her shoulders. Holding her head high, she marched back into the dining room.

"Hey, Wall Street. That was pretty good work you did tonight—for a newbie."

"Hah, hah, Cruz." Shane Kavanaugh snorted as the ambulance rolled to a stop in the New Suffolk regional community medical building. "I left New York six months ago. I'm an EMT." Step one of his life plan—complete. Step two... He couldn't wait to start paramedic classes in the fall.

Duncan Cruz rested his hands on the steering wheel and faced Shane. "Gotta say, it's a heck of a career change."

Shane viewed the switch as refocusing on his original goal—a career in the medical field—something he'd wanted to do from the time he was six years old and his father, Victor, first got sick. Dad would have preferred he join Turner Kavanaugh Construction, the company his father had started with his best friend more than thirty years ago—but Shane was sure Dad would be proud of him for being true to himself—even if he hadn't lived long enough to see the man he'd become. Above all else, Victor had wanted his kids to be happy.

New York had never made him happy. He'd tried like hell for a long time to believe it would, but he couldn't fool himself any longer.

The money was great. He couldn't deny that. He'd been like a kid in a candy store buying every treat he could find in the beginning. Having cash to spare had been a powerful draw for a guy who… Well, while he couldn't classify his family as poor—not by any stretch of the imagination—but growing up, there definitely hadn't been money in the Kavanaugh home for frivolous things.

What was the old saying? *Money can't buy you happiness.* Yes, that was it. Whoever came up with that saying was spot-on.

"Let's just say the city life's not for me." He missed walking down Main Street and greeting his fellow neighbors by name. Missed the sense of community that came with small-town living.

"You're a small-town boy through and through, huh?" Cruz let out a roar of laughter.

Absolutely. "Hey. I like it here in New Suffolk."

Life in Massachusetts suited Shane just fine. Always had. He never needed to pretend to be something— someone—he wasn't. He was good enough—as is. He'd finally realized that.

Duncan pulled the keys from the ignition. "Hey, wanna go down to Donahue's and shoot some pool after we restock the ambulance?"

He nodded. "Yeah, sure. Sounds good. Loser buys the first round."

Duncan grinned. "I guess you'll be buying then."

Shane shot him a disparaging glance. "We'll see about that." He jumped out of the ambulance and strode to the stockroom.

Thirty minutes later Shane drove his F-150 up to Donahue's Irish Pub. As always, the place was rocking on a Saturday night. He hoped they wouldn't have to wait too long for a pool table. He pulled into a spot in the back of the lot and hopped out of the truck.

Snow fluttered from the clear night sky as he exited the driver's seat. The first day of spring might officially arrive in twenty days, but it felt as if the warmer weather would never get here. Shane zipped his bomber jacket, shoved his hands in his coat pockets and picked up his pace as he strode toward the entrance.

Loud music accosted him as he stepped inside. A group of local musicians rocked out on the stage in the back of the room. The song ended and the singer announced the band would take a thirty-minute break. Shane strode down the short narrow hall that led to the bar area.

He scanned the room. A woman standing near the front entrance caught his attention. Shane studied her as she moved in his direction.

Tall and thin with long dark curly hair, her hips swayed ever so slightly as she moved through the throng of people. She wasn't Hollywood gorgeous, but he found her quiet beauty attractive nonetheless. Who was she?

She disappeared from his view.

Shane searched the crowd for a few minutes but couldn't find her anywhere.

"Excuse me," a female said.

He jerked his attention toward the voice. His mystery woman stood in front of him. Tonight was his lucky night.

"Could you please move?" The woman offered a

winsome smile. "I need to leave." She pointed to the door behind him. "I can't get by."

"Oh, I'm sorry." He grinned and stepped aside.

"Thank you." Her gaze connected with his and she stiffened. "Shane."

How did she know his name? He scrutinized her face, then recognition slowly hit him.

Holy hell.

"Layla?" *No way.* The Layla Williams he remembered had shoulder-length light brown hair. Not long, dark, silky curls and certainly not the sexy curves this woman sported.

"Yes. It's me." Her gaze darted around the space.

"It's been a while." At least a few years.

"Yes," she agreed.

Why wouldn't she look at him? "How are you doing?" he asked.

"Fine. Um... You?" came her clipped reply.

Nothing had changed over the years. The rich Manhattan socialite still wanted nothing to do with a townie. Would she be as standoffish if she viewed his bank statement? Most women found him—his portfolio, he mentally corrected—quite attractive.

His wealth may have secured admittance into New York's upper echelon, Melinda *had* married him, after all, but admittance and acceptance were two different animals. He'd learned that the hard way.

"I'm surprised to see you." He couldn't hide the disdain in his voice.

"I'm...hanging out with some friends."

Here? Shane's jaw almost hit the ground. Donahue's

wasn't a dive, but… He'd never have guessed a Williams would enter such an establishment. They'd frequented the Bay Beach Club during those years they'd summered here. He ought to know. He'd waited on her and her family often enough over the years.

"At least I was. I'm heading over to my restaurant now."

He'd heard she'd purchased her grandfather's place when he retired.

"I opened La Cabane de La Mer last summer." A look of pride flashed across her expression.

She'd have been better off sticking with a name for her restaurant that sounded less uptight, pretentious. Something with wider appeal, in his opinion. "How is your restaurant doing?" He'd noticed fewer cars in the parking lot when he passed by on the way home each day. Then again, many of the businesses in town suffered from a turndown in commerce during the winter months, when tourism tended to slow in the coastal towns.

Layla flashed a wide smile that stole the breath from him. The way it lit up the room, and transformed her face from…well, she'd always been beautiful, but the warmth and joy radiating from her now jolted through him like a bolt of lightning.

"It's great." She glanced at her watch. "But I have to go."

Same old Layla. A bitter smile crossed his face. "Of course." He gestured for her to pass by.

As she walked by him, murmuring a distracted "Bye," and disappeared outside, it was as though he'd imagined the transformation of a few moments ago. An odd feeling of disappointment shot through him before he shrugged it off and continued down the hall.

Shane walked into the bar and peered around. Several patrons sat in the high-back chairs along the length of the long glossy wood bar to his right. He spotted Levi Turner at the far end. Walking over, he clapped his friend on the shoulder. "Hey, man. What's up? How did you get out of the house tonight? I thought you have Noah on Saturday nights."

Levi turned sideways in the chair and faced him. "I usually do, but he's with his mother tonight. I'm supposed to meet Cooper here for a beer, but he's late."

"How is your little brother?" Shane waved at the bartender and he came toward him.

"I'm fine." Cooper Turner walked over and grabbed the seat next to Levi. "Sorry I'm late."

"No problem." Levi slid a pint toward his brother. "It might be a little warm now."

Cooper snorted.

"What can I get you, Shane?" the bartender asked.

"I'll take the New Suffolk IPA, Ben."

"Me, too," Cooper added and shoved the warm glass of beer aside.

Ben nodded, grabbed a couple of frosted glasses and headed to the tap a few feet away.

Shane scanned the room but couldn't find Duncan anywhere. They'd left the EMS building at the same time. He must have stopped somewhere along the way.

He directed his attention to Levi and Cooper. "So—"

Someone slammed into him from behind. Shane

whirled around and caught an older man before he landed on the ground.

"Sorry 'bout that," the man grumbled.

Shane stared into the man's vacant gaze. Something about his weathered features seemed familiar.

"Another bourbon, Ben," the man called.

"Not a chance. You've had enough, Gary. You're shut off."

"Gary Rawlins?" Shane's gaze widened.

Gary jerked his blurry gaze to him, and snarled, "Yeah. What of it?"

No wonder the man had looked familiar. This was his best friend's father. He held out his hand. "Shane Kavanaugh."

Gary did a double take and a small smile crossed his once handsome face. "Well, I'll be damned." He pumped Shane's hand. "Haven't seen you in years." He wobbled, but straightened himself before he fell. Clapping Shane on the shoulder, he said, "Mind ordering me a bourbon?"

Shane's mouth fell open. "How about I call you a cab instead?"

Ben returned, and set full mugs down in front of him and Cooper. "Already done. The cab will be here any minute."

"I'm not ready to go home," Gary objected.

"Okay, but you know the rules." Ben pointed to the door. "You're banned from this place if you don't leave when I tell you."

Gary groused some more as he made his way to the exit.

"Sorry about that," Ben gestured to Gary's retreating form.

"No problem." Shane waved off Ben's concern. "Does this happen often?" Jax's father tended to indulge on certain occasions, but he'd never seem him this bad before.

"Often enough." Levi snorted.

Ben shook his head. "We've had an arrangement with the cab company for years."

"Ever since Jax left town," Cooper added. "You ever see him when you lived in Manhattan?"

"Sometimes." Shane nodded. "When he was around, which wasn't much."

"Who would have thought one of New Suffolk's own would make it big?" Levi said.

"Rachel and I went to one of his shows last year, when his photos were featured at a gallery in Boston," Cooper added.

"Hey, look who just walked in." Cooper pointed to three women who stood by the front entrance.

"Who are they?" Shane asked.

"The middle one with the blond hair is big brother's fiancée," Levi scoffed.

Cooper elbowed Levi in the side. "Would you just stop already?" To Shane he said, "Her name is Isabelle."

Shane's eyes widened. "Nick is engaged? When did this happen?"

"Yesterday." Levi snorted and shook his head. "Worse—"

Cooper cut in before Levi could continue. "Not all

marriages end up in the toilet. You just need to meet the right person." He jerked his head to Shane, a back-me-up-here expression on his face.

"Don't look at me for confirmation." He wouldn't be making his way down the aisle again. Not in this lifetime. *That's for sure.*

"Oh, come on." Cooper rolled his eyes skyward. "Don't tell me you're a card-carrying member of the He Man Woman Haters club, like my brother here." Cooper gestured to Levi.

Levi snorted. "I'd say the answer to that is no, given he was checking out a hot little number not more than five minutes ago."

"What are you talking about?" he asked.

Levi leaned back in his chair and shot a challenging glance in his direction. "You're going to deny you were checking out Layla Williams?"

Shane opened his mouth but Levi jumped in before he could say anything.

"I saw you when you came in. I waved, but you obviously didn't see me." Levi arched a brow and flashed a smug smile. "You were otherwise engaged."

"Didn't you used to have a wicked crush on her when we were kids?" Cooper asked.

Levi smirked. "Oh yeah. I forgot about that. You had it bad for her."

"I don't know what you're talking about." *Lie much?* Because yeah, he'd just told a whopper. Yes, he'd fallen hook, line and sinker for Layla all those years ago. That fourteen-year-old boy had been naive enough to believe their backgrounds wouldn't matter. *Yeah, right*. Lifting his mug to his mouth, he swallowed a gulp of his beer.

"Not much has changed, has it?" Levi nudged him in the ribs. "She wouldn't give you the time of day back then and it looked like tonight was no different."

"Whatever." He gave a dismissive gesture. Shane could care less. He might find Layla attractive, but he sure as hell wasn't interested in pursuing her. He'd had his fill of Manhattan socialites, enough to last the rest of this lifetime and into the next. "I'm focused on my career right now. I'm not looking for a relationship."

"Amen to that." Levi lifted his mug and clinked it with his.

"Oh, come on," Cooper insisted.

He shook his head. Love wouldn't last. It never did. He ought to know.

When it ended… His gut twisted. *Never again*.

The reward wasn't worth any amount of risk.

Chapter Two

Layla woke on Sunday morning to the bright light blazing into her bedroom. She jumped out of bed and walked to the window. Sunshine glowed in a cloudless blue sky. A few people meandered along Main Street, even at this early hour.

Although she enjoyed this view of the town green from her place above the Coffee Palace, she missed the serenity of waking to the sounds of surf crashing on shore and the waves rolling in from the sea. Layla wished she could have continued to live in the second-story apartment above La Cabane de La Mer. Lord knew the space would have been more than enough for her, and she could have saved the monthly rent she paid to live here, but the private lender she'd used to secure the loan required to finance the restaurant renovations wouldn't allow it.

She glanced around the room. For now, the gray Ikea modular couch and black lacquer rectangle table would suit her fine. Not to mention the perks of living above a fabulous coffee shop and the friendship she'd found with Elle, the woman who lived across the hall, and Abby, the coffee shop owner.

Layla turned from her view and headed down the short hall to the bathroom. After a quick shower and dressing in warm clothes, she descended the exterior back staircase and walked around to the front of the building once she reached the parking lot. She walked inside and stepped up to the counter.

"Good morning, Layla. Oh, my. Do I have something to tell you. Things got quite interesting after you left Donahue's last night." Abby tucked a lock of titian hair behind her ear. She shuffled to the display case containing a selection of confections.

How lucky was she to have been inducted into the sisterhood? For the first time in her life, she had steadfast female friends she could rely on. Although truth be told, she was still getting used to the gal pal thing. Her sister was the outgoing one of the two of them. Zara loved to party and be surrounded by swarms of people, while she'd always preferred to be with Gramps in his kitchen.

Gramps never thought she was weird because she'd rather cook than go hang out at the mall or get her nails done. He never shoved her in front of a boy she'd crushed on and laughed when she'd almost lost her lunch trying to talk to him.

While she might have outgrown the nausea, her cautious, wary side still made frequent appearances—but she was working on that thanks to these wonderful, supportive, funny, loving women.

Layla grinned. "Do tell."

"You know who," Abby pointed to the back room, "finally plucked up the courage to ask that cute guy she'd been drooling over, for the last few weeks, to dance."

"By you know who, she means me." Elle sashayed in from the kitchen. Her long blond hair was piled on the top of her head in a haphazard bun. The hairstyle added a good four inches to Elle's petite stature.

"So…" Layla grinned, enjoying the comradery. "What happened after you danced?"

Abby let out a low whistle. "Just the dancing was pretty hot. The two of them were stuck together like Velcro. And that kiss…" She fanned herself.

"Get your mind out of the gutter." Elle's cheeks flamed.

"Someone had a good night. That's all I'm sayin'," Abby retorted. "Anything to eat today?" she asked Layla.

Layla studied the trays of sweets. "I can't decide which one I want. Surprise me."

Wax paper in hand, Abby reached inside the display case and plucked a figure-eight Danish from one of the trays on the top shelf. "Cherries and cheese okay?"

She nodded. "Sounds yummy."

"Excuse me." A short woman with a chin-length brown bob appeared.

Elle glanced over her shoulder. "Oh, hey. This is Mia. She just started here today."

Something about the woman seemed vaguely familiar, but Layla couldn't place a finger on what. "Hi, Mia." Layla extended her hand over the counter. "Have we met before?"

Mia cocked her head to the side and scrutinized Layla's face. "I was just wondering the same thing."

"Maybe you two have bumped into each other here." Abby moved to the coffeepot and filled a large to-go cup. She added cream and sugar and handed it to Layla. "She and her three girls come in on the weekends along with Mia's mom, Jane Kavanaugh."

Shane. She remembered their brief exchange at Donahue's the other night. Yep. She couldn't have made a bigger fool of herself if she'd tried. The minute she'd recognized him… Can you say shy fourteen-year-old with a schoolgirl crush complete with sweaty palms and a topsy-turvy stomach? At least she hadn't lost her lunch. *Thank You, God, for small mercies.*

She'd annoyed him, for sure. *No news there.* He'd always found her irritating. *Poor little rich girl.* Oh, he'd never called her that to her face, but she knew damn well he believed it, according to some of the other locals who'd worked at the Bay Beach Club those years her family summered in New Suffolk.

"Layla?" Elle's voice cut into her thoughts.

"Sorry. I remember now," she said to Mia. "Your mom introduced us here at the Coffee Palace a few months ago—right before Christmas. The five of you had stopped in for a treat after taking your daughters to see Santa at the community center. It's nice to see you again."

Recognition dawned in Mia's gaze. "Right. It's nice to see you, too."

The bell above the door chimed. A tall man entered the shop.

"Shane." Mia's eyes widened. "What are you doing here?"

Layla whirled around. Lord, it was as if her thoughts had conjured him.

Shane swaggered over to where they stood. His big grin sent a tingle down her spine and made her insides go soft and mushy.

What was wrong with her this morning? So what if Shane had a great smile? He meant nothing to her.

"Ladies." He gave a brief nod of his head. "I'm here to support my big sister."

"By all means." Abby stepped aside and motioned for Mia to replace her at the counter.

"Hi, Shane." Layla's words came out in a rush.

He jerked his attention to her. "Layla. Hello." He gave her a polite smile.

A smile was good. So much better than the frown he always wore around her all those summers ago. "It's nice to see you again." Layla sucked in a deep breath. She wouldn't freeze up again. "I mean I haven't seen you in years and now it's been twice in two days." She gave a nervous laugh.

"Right." He eyed her as if she were delusional.

First, she couldn't string two words together, and now she couldn't stop talking. *Bumbling fool.*

Shane turned his attention to his sister. "I'll take a large black coffee, one of those giant cookies with M&M's and an apple fritter."

"Hungry much?" Mia aimed a smirk at her brother.

"Ha, ha. The second pastry is for Mom. She's outside." He jerked his head toward the entrance. "I ran into her in the parking lot, but she got a call. I said I'd order for her."

The chime sounded again and Jane Kavanaugh stepped in. "Good morning, everyone."

"Hi, Jane," Abby and Elle said at the same time.

"Hello." Layla smiled. Would Shane's mother remember her?

"Layla." Jane gave her a hug. "It's so nice to see you again."

Shane frowned. "You two know each other?"

"Of course we do. I've known Layla for years. I used to see her all the time when she visited her grandparents."

Layla prayed Jane had never suspected the truth about those occasions—that she'd arranged to run into Jane on purpose—so she could find out how Shane was doing and what he was up to.

Yes, she'd crushed on Shane something fierce in those days. Heat crept up her neck and Layla suspected her cheeks had turned red.

That was a long time ago.

"Do you want something to drink, Mom?" Mia asked. "Shane only ordered one coffee."

"No. I've got a mug in my car." Abby rang up the

order while Mia filled a cup and placed each sweet in a paper bag.

Jane picked up her order. "I'm off to run a few errands."

"Bye," Layla called.

"Me, too." Shane grabbed his bag and cup and turned to the door.

"Have a great day." Layla winced when he just stared at her. She breathed a sigh of relief when he exited the shop. "I've got to get going, too. Take care." Coffee and Danish in hand, Layla headed toward the exit.

"Wait a minute," Elle called. "I almost forgot. Are you in for tonight?"

Layla turned to face the women. Their weekly Sunday night poker game. Those cutthroat women took the game seriously. Layla couldn't blame them. Not with such high stakes at risk. Reese's Peanut Butter Cups Miniatures, Hershey's Nuggets, and the occasional fun-size Hershey Bars thrown in for good measure. "Heck, yeah. I can't wait."

"How about you?" Elle turned her attention to Abby.

"Absolutely. And cousin or not, you get none of my winnings," Abby replied to Elle.

Layla cocked her head and jutted her chin. "You think you're going to win, do you? We'll see about that."

Abby crooked a smug smile. "Yes, we will."

"What about you, Mia? Care to join us for a little fun?" Elle asked.

"Are you sure? I wouldn't want to intrude."

"Positive," Abby responded. "The more the merrier."

"I agree," Layla added.

Mia smiled. "I'd love to. Let me see if I can get my mother to watch the girls for me. I'll give her a call during my break and let you know."

"Great." Elle gave a little wave and strode to the back room. Mia followed.

"See you later," Layla called over her shoulder as she walked to the exit.

Layla stepped outside. The blazing sun glinted off the white snow covering the town green. She sipped her coffee, passing the new boutique that had opened right after Thanksgiving, the local courthouse and the police station as she made her way through town.

She turned right when she reached the public beach access. The peaceful tranquility of the waves crashing on shore calmed her mind and body. Who cared if most of the sand was covered with a foot of snow? Not her. She proceeded down the boardwalk and trudged through the gleaming white snow toward the ocean. High tide had washed away some of Mother Nature's white blanket, leaving a strip of sand visible about two feet from the water's edge.

Sipping her coffee, she meandered along the narrow path taking care to avoid the water to her right and the snow to her left.

The pavilion came into view. A lone man stood inside; his elbows propped up on the railing. He stared out at the waves crashing on shore.

Shane. Layla recognized him as she approached. She

studied him from this vantage point. Dressed in jeans and a hooded sweatshirt, he cut an imposing figure.

High cheekbones, a rugged square cut jaw. He'd always been handsome, although her fourteen-year-old self wouldn't have used that term to describe his tall, lanky frame, his wavy brown hair that was just a little too shaggy to be considered clean-cut, and those mesmerizing sapphire-blue eyes. *Don't forget his smile.* It had made her innocent heart slam in her chest. If she were honest, it still did.

Shane spotted her. His piercing gaze bore down on her, scrutinizing, assessing.

Something flashed between them. Intense, fiery, it threatened to consume her.

She blinked. Shane was gone when her eyes fluttered open.

Her mind whirled, a chaotic swirl of emotion.

What had just happened between them?

Shane glanced at his watch. Ten more minutes and he'd need to leave for work. He munched the last of his cookie as he stared out at the sea and breathed in the crisp clean air.

A man raced along the beach chasing after two young children who laughed and played in the snow. It reminded him of the walks he used to take with his dad when he was a kid. They'd stop at the Coffee Palace, where Dad would get a coffee and he'd get a cookie. They'd walk along the beach and end up here, at one of the tables in the pavilion. Shane would tell him about his week at school and Dad would tell him about whose house they were renovating or building and how much he looked forward to Shane joining the family business one day.

Shane smiled into the wind. Despite what he'd told his father about wanting to work in the hospital so he could make people better, like the people who'd made Dad better—at least they had in the beginning—he'd taught him how to wield a hammer and by the time Shane reached his early teens, he'd accompany his father on small jobs.

He caught sight of someone else approaching in his peripheral vision. Layla. Shane shook his head. Leave it to her to come along and disrupt his thoughts.

Shane blew out a breath as she continued walking. He studied her face now that she was closer. How could he have forgotten who she was? She still looked like the girl he'd met in her grandfather's kitchen all those years ago.

His mind drifted back to that day.

"Boys, would you like some lemonade?" Mrs. Williams stepped over the short stack of two-by-four planks on the floor as she entered the bedroom in the upstairs apartment above the restaurant.

Shane glanced over at her as he held a piece of Sheetrock in place while his father tacked the gypsum board to the new frame they'd just made.

"I've got fresh-baked cookies, too," Mrs. Williams added. "They're right out of the oven."

"You guys go ahead," Dad said to him and Levi. "Take a break. Just be back in fifteen minutes."

"Follow me," Mrs. Williams said.

They walked into the living room. Shane marveled at the paintings that hung in gold frames on the walls and the decorative...what had his father called the large vases that sat atop the glossy wood tables? Urns. Yeah, that's what they were. He'd never seen anything so fancy in his life.

"It's this way, boys." *Mrs. Williams walked into the kitchen.*

Shane's mouth fell open when he spotted the young girl about his age standing with a tray of chocolate-chip cookies in her hand. Her hair was tied back in a ponytail and freckles dotted her nose. His stomach flip-flopped all over the place. She had to be the prettiest girl he'd ever seen.

"Boys, this is my granddaughter. Layla, this is Mr. Turner's son Levi." *She pointed to her right.* "And Mr. Kavanaugh's son Shane." *She gestured left to him.* "They're helping with the renovations to the bedroom we're redoing for you and your sister to stay in when you come here for visits."

"Hey." *Levi grabbed two cookies from the plate on the counter and a glass of lemonade.*

"Hi." *Shane smiled. He couldn't take his gaze off her.*

"These are really good," *Levi mumbled.*

"See, I told you, Layla," *Mrs. Williams said.*

"You made the cookies?" *he asked.*

Layla nodded.

Shane reached for one and bit into the gooey treat. "They're awesome."

Layla's cheeks turned bright red, but she smiled at him.

A rush of warmth flooded through him. His pulse went through the roof.

He smiled back.

Shane blinked. Why was he wasting time on memories that didn't matter anymore? He returned his focus to the surf.

Layla's gaze connected with his.

Something zipped between them, powerful and strong; his heart pounded even faster for a moment.

Shane inhaled a lungful of air and blew it out slowly as he tried to steady his erratic breathing. Why was he allowing her to affect him this way? Like Levi had said yesterday, she hadn't given him the time of day back then and nothing had changed as far as he could see.

It's nice to see you again. Her words flashed into his mind and the genuine smile on her face...

There went his traitorous heart again.

Shane banished the *what-ifs* banging around in his head. He'd already learned the hard way; girls like her brought nothing but heartache.

Shane strode into the empty locker room at the regional medical building and Duncan followed.

"I can't wait to get home and put up my feet for a couple of hours. It's been a long day." Duncan grabbed his jacket from his locker and shrugged it on.

Shane nodded. "You got that right." Three trips to the hospital over the last eight hours had kept them busy.

"See you later." Duncan exited the locker room.

Shane finished changing into his street clothes.

After packing his uniform into his duffel bag, he slung the strap over his shoulder and headed toward the exit to the parking lot.

He spotted a light on in Mark Burke's office as he made his way down the dimly lit hall. What was the EMS director doing here on a Sunday evening? Shane started to knock but held back when he heard voices.

"I'm well aware of the limited town budget," Mark said.

"You keep saying that," someone else responded.

Shane stopped and listened. The voice sounded familiar, but he couldn't connect the voice with a face.

"We can't afford to lose anyone, Lionel."

Was that Mayor White? Had to be. There wasn't another Lionel in New Suffolk as far as he knew.

"We're already operating the EMS at minimum staffing levels. If we lose even one person, we can't properly serve the community," Mark added.

"We may not have a choice. You know the EMS budget relies heavily on donations and other revenues generated," the mayor said.

"We've got the gala fundraiser coming up in roughly six weeks," Mark responded. "I'm sure we'll be able to raise the funds we need."

"You'd better hope so," Lionel said.

Shane sucked in a breath. Would Mark really have to cut personnel if the upcoming gala couldn't generate enough money? Damn. He could be one of those people. *Last in, first out.* That's the way it usually worked—in the business world. How many times had he seen it happen to his friends on Wall Street? Enough to know what happened when times got tough.

"Duncan and the rest of the volunteer committee for the gala are meeting tonight at seven here in the medical building. You're more than welcome to attend and see for yourself how the planning is going," Mark offered. "Better yet, you can offer your services. The committee can always use extra people."

If Duncan needed help, Shane was about to volunteer.

The community college Shane wanted to attend next semester required six months of EMT on-the-job experience as a prerequisite for acceptance into their paramedic program. Sure, there were other programs in the state that didn't make such requirements, but they were already full for the fall.

If he lost this job now...

No. He'd worked hard to get this far and he wasn't about to let his dream slip away now.

Shane would do what needed to be done to ensure he kept this position. No matter what.

Have a last-minute committee meeting for the gala this evening. Can't make our weekly game after all. Layla sent the text to Elle. Grabbing her purse, she slid from the car. A gust of wind blew and she shivered. Zipping her jacket, Layla quickened her pace as she strode toward the entrance of the EMS building.

Stepping into the empty main hall, she stopped in front of the wall containing the years-of-service plaques. She still got a kick out of seeing her grandfather's plaque on the top row with the five other founding members.

"I remember working with Joe when I first started here. Your grandfather was a great paramedic."

She jumped and whirled around to face the newcomer. "Oh. Hi, Mark."

"Sorry. I didn't mean to startle you," the EMS director said.

"No. That's okay." She gestured to the wall behind her. "I like seeing his picture up there." She was proud of his contributions to the community. Even after he'd retired from the EMS department, he'd continued his support.

"I see you're following in his footsteps."

Brows furrowed; she cocked her head to the side. "What are you talking about?"

"Allowing us to use your restaurant for the fundraiser. Joe hosted at least one EMS event a year when he owned the place. I can't wait to see what you've done now that you've taken over."

She beamed a warm smile at him. "Don't wait until the ball. Come by anytime. Tell your friends, too."

"Will do."

"We should get going." She gestured down the hall to where the community rooms were located. "The fundraiser meeting will start soon."

"I can't make it tonight. I have a family commitment. It was nice seeing you, Layla. Thanks again for helping with this event. It's people like you and the rest of the committee that make it possible for us to raise the money we need to better service the district."

"You're welcome. I'm glad to help." Giving was

important. A responsibility as far as her parents and grandparents were concerned, for everyone. If you can't give financially, find another way, Gramps would say.

How could she have lost track of those values over the last few years? Antoine's image appeared in her head. The fact that he didn't share her beliefs should have been a red flag. Yet she'd dismissed the facts, choosing to see what she wanted. *Foolish, all right.* Layla wouldn't make that mistake again.

She continued down the hall and stopped at an open door on the right. The fundraiser team sat inside on either side of two long banquet tables which stood side by side. She grabbed the last open chair.

Her eyes widened when she caught a glimpse of the man to her right. What was Shane Kavanaugh doing here? He seemed as surprised to see her as she him.

Duncan Cruz rose and called the meeting to order. "Thanks for coming, everyone. We're a little less than a month and a half from our event. I have something I need to share with you, but first, I want to introduce a new committee member." Duncan gestured to Shane. "For those of you who don't already know him, this is Shane Kavanaugh. He joined the department about a month ago."

Mr. New York Stock Exchange was an emergency medical technician? *Like Gramps?* No. That couldn't be right. He wasn't anything like her beloved grandfather.

He was a Wall Street Wolf. Wasn't he?

Shane cringed when Layla walked into the room. Wasn't it just his luck she'd be involved with the benefit? He couldn't catch a break.

He straightened and gave a little wave to acknowledge Duncan's introduction.

"Let's get started." Duncan explained the situation with the town budget and how they needed to generate as much revenue from this event as possible. "I'm looking for ideas we can easily implement since we don't have much planning time left."

Hal Smith raised his hand. "What if we changed the seating to family style instead of individual tables?"

Shane nodded. "Great idea. We can seat more people that way, which means we can sell more tickets."

"Can we do that, Layla?" Duncan asked.

"Sure. I don't have long tables, but we can string several of the small ones together and create the same effect."

Duncan grinned. "I like it. What else?"

"What if we do a themed event?" Layla said.

Duncan pursed his lips as if considering. "What did you have in mind?"

"We'll go upscale. Black tie for the men, fancy dresses for the women."

Faith nudged her husband. "Looks like I'm going shopping."

The group chuckled.

Layla grinned. "We'll have fairy lights, gold candelabras on the tables. Lots of glitz and glamour."

"We decorated the fire trucks with white lights for the parade last Christmas," Quinn Cain said. "I'm sure the chief will allow us to use them."

"Sophisticated Blooms can donate flower arrangements," Sophie Bloom added.

A round of *yeses* and *sounds goods* ensued.

Layla's eyes lit with excitement. "We can even do an ice sculpture in the main entry."

An ice sculpture? Seriously? Talk about over-the-top.

The rest of the group agreed with him if their silences were anything to go by.

"You don't have to answer now." Layla laced her fingers together and rested her hands on the table. "Just think about it."

He rolled his eyes skyward. Man, she was just too much.

"While I love your enthusiasm," Duncan started, "and I'm not saying we shouldn't go ahead and snazz things up a bit—because I think we should—our ultimate goal is to generate as much cash as we can. I'm not sure a themed event would bring in the extra money we need."

"Not to mention we'd exceed our budget to pull it off." Faith sighed. "I'm still shopping for a fancy dress." She winked at Layla.

"Me, too." Sophie smiled. "And I'm still willing to donate the flower arrangements."

"I'll string the lights," Quinn added.

"Great." Duncan nodded. "What else can we do?"

"What about a silent auction?" Hal suggested.

"That's always a good moneymaker," Shane agreed.

"We can get donations from local businesses," Sue added.

"I can make that work," Layla confirmed. "We have plenty of space."

"Now you're talking." Duncan gave two thumbs up.

"Sue and I will work together." Hal pointed to his wife sitting next to him. "But we'll need other volunteers to help."

Shane raised his hand along with several other members of the group.

"Tina and Yvonne." Duncan pointed to the two women who sat closest to him. "Sally and Tom." He indicated two others who'd raised their hands. He scanned the group. He pointed to him. "Shane. You team up with Layla."

Work with Layla? For crying out loud. Can't catch a break, indeed. He slanted his gaze in her direction. She seemed less than thrilled with their pairing. Shane straightened his shoulders and held his head high. Well, that was too damned bad. He was as good a partner to work with as any of the others in the room.

Deal with it. He would.

So, they'd spend a few hours together collecting donations. No big deal. The fundraiser would generate the extra revenue they needed. He'd keep his job.

What could go wrong?

Chapter Three

Layla glanced at her watch. They closed at nine on Friday evenings in the winter—no use staying open when the whole town shut down early—but she'd leave the front entrance open so Zara could get in.

Something was up with her sister and Layla was worried.

Zara's call last night had set her on edge when she'd told her she was on her way to New Suffolk. This week should have been a Zoom call according to their schedule of weekly remote meetings and one face to face a month, but she'd insisted on meeting in person.

Even more bizarre, she'd pressed Layla to meet today. They always held their in-person meetings on Saturdays. That way Zara wouldn't miss a day of work.

And the thing with her showing up here late this afternoon and insisting they perform the review immediately was *really weird*. She'd seemed…almost panicky when Layla couldn't drop what she was doing and accommodate the request.

"Layla," her sous-chef called.

"Coming." She hoisted the case of Château Lafite Rothschild Pauillac into her arms and strode toward the bar. Lifting the four remaining bottles from the cardboard box, she set each one atop the glossy wood surface.

"Oh, here you are." Olivia approached. "The kitchen's all set. I'm heading out now."

"Okay, thanks. See you tomorrow." Layla brushed a stray lock of curly hair from her sweaty face.

"Oh, the mailman delivered a certified letter earlier. Couldn't find you so I signed for it and left it on the chair in your office."

That was weird. Who would send her a certified letter? "Okay, thanks for letting me know." Layla headed down the back hall toward her office. She flicked on the light. Sure enough, a large manila envelope sat propped against the back of her brown leather swivel desk chair.

Her brows furrowed as she read the letterhead in the upper left corner. It was from the private lender who'd issued the loan she'd taken out to finance opening the restaurant, using the mansion as collateral. Grabbing the envelope, she tore it open and dropped into the cool seat.

Layla removed the letter and scanned the first page. Her eyes bugged out. "What the hell?"

"Hey, Layla. Where are you?" her sister called.

She rushed out of her office, through the empty restaurant to the front entrance to meet her. "What is this?" Layla clenched the document in her hand.

"What is what?" Zara asked.

Layla thrust the document at Zara. "Notice of Default." She shook her head. "I don't understand. They're going to force me to sell the mansion to pay off the loan in full if I can't make the loan current by the end of the first week of April." She lifted her gaze to Zara's. "Why would they believe the loan isn't current?" Her finances might be a little tight, but she hadn't missed a payment.

Zara wouldn't answer. She just stood there with a deer-in-the-headlights expression on her face.

Layla sucked in a lungful of air and tried to relax. Yelling at her sister wasn't going to straighten out this mistake. Zara was obviously as surprised by this as Layla. They'd figure it out together.

She walked into the bar. Setting the document aside, she pulled two wineglasses from the rack and set them atop the glossy bar top. "Red or white," she asked when Zara sat in a chair on the opposite side of her.

"Doesn't matter," Zara grunted.

Layla opened a bottle of her favorite Bordeaux and poured two glasses.

"I'm sorry—" She and Zara spoke at the same time.

Layla heaved out a sigh. "Let me go first. I shouldn't have yelled at you. I'm just…in shock, I guess." She drew in a deep breath and let it out slowly. "Do you have any idea what's going on? How could the lender make such a mistake?"

"It's not a mistake." Zara's voice held a note of panic.

Layla stiffened. Her eyes went wide. "Excuse me? What do you mean? There must be some kind of processing error." If there wasn't... Nausea churned in her stomach and burned a path up her throat.

Zara scrubbed her hands over her face. "I couldn't cover the loan amount due in January or February."

The shaking started in her hands and spread like wildfire throughout her body until she shook from head to toes. But she tried to keep calm. "Why would you miss two payments?" How could that happen? She would have noticed the discrepancies during their weekly finance reviews except... An image of her sister's washed-out face formed in her head. "Oh, my God. You've been hiding this from me. Were you even sick, or was it all a sham so you could keep the truth from me?"

Tears formed in Zara's eyes.

Layla rubbed at her temples and started to pace back and forth behind the bar. "Why would you do such a thing?"

Zara's head lowered and her voice shook when she spoke. "I wasn't... I didn't think..."

She marched over to where Zara sat. Her hands clenched into tight fists. "Why couldn't you make the payments?"

"You're not making enough money."

"Are you kidding me?" Okay, yes. The tourists who'd filled her dining room to capacity every night last summer had departed at the end of the season, but still...

"These days, you barely make enough to cover day-to-day operating expenses." Zara sounded as if she were dealing with a stubborn child who refused to listen.

The image of a nearly empty dining room popped into her head. Her shoulders slumped. "Why didn't you tell me when we missed the first payment?"

"You didn't seem worried when things slowed down after the holidays and I figured we'd make up the missed payment in February."

"But we didn't, and still you said nothing. And how the hell would I make it up in the off-season, of all times?" A heavy weight settled in her chest making it hard to breathe. "For God's sake. You agreed to manage the finances, Zara. I *trusted* you."

The color drained from Zara's face. "I know. I'm trying, but managing *your* restaurant isn't anything like what I did for Gramps, or what I do for the nonprofit. You have so many more moving parts to juggle, new suppliers every week. Just when I believe I'm caught up, you surprise me with another invoice to pay. That coupled with the fact that I hadn't anticipated the steep decline in business in January and February meant I wound up short when the loan payments were due."

"I'm sorry. I really am." Zara's crushed spirit tore at her insides. "I spoke to the lender yesterday. They told me about the letter. I wanted to tell you myself this afternoon. It's why I came up."

Layla scrubbed her hands over her face. She didn't know what to say.

"Please don't hate me," Zara pleaded.

Her heart squeezed. This was her sister—her best friend through thick and thin—not archenemy number one. She wouldn't have made it through those initial days after her split from Antoine without Zara's love and support.

Lord, what a mess they'd made of this.

Zara wiped tears from her eyes. "I never thought it would come to this."

"But it has." Her breaths came in short, sharp gasps. Everything she'd worked for. All her dreams. Gone.

Done. At last. Shane yawned. He couldn't wait to hit the hay. He pushed the door open and exited the EMS building. Stars twinkled in the dark sky and the full moon negated the need for lights as he strode through the parking lot to his truck.

Once there, he tossed his duffel bag on the passenger seat and hopped inside. Shane pulled out of the parking lot and headed east. He drove through the now silent town and turned left at the light and headed toward home.

The bright lights shining at La Cabane de La Mer surprised him. He wouldn't have guessed the restaurant would be open at this hour. Of all the people on the gala committee, wasn't it just his luck he'd end up paired with Layla? Shane blew out a harsh breath. Now that his work schedule was set for the next two weeks, he needed to speak with her and set up a time they could collect the rest of the silent auction donations. Now was as good a time as any. He made a U-turn and headed back.

The parking lot was empty when he pulled in. Maybe he'd been wrong, and the restaurant was closed? He was here, so he may as well check. Shane hopped out of his truck and walked toward the entrance.

Silence greeted him when he stepped inside. "Hello? Is anyone here?" A loud crash came from the room to his left. "Who's there?"

"We're closed," a female voice yelled.

He moved toward the sound but couldn't find anyone. "Hello," he called again.

"I said we're closed." The sound came from behind the bar.

"Layla?" Shane walked over and peered over the marble countertop. She sat in a heap on the floor with three broken wine bottles beside her and spilled red wine on the floor. He rushed to her side. "Oh, no. What happened?"

She shot an accusing glare at him. "It scared the heck out of me when I heard your voice and I knocked over the bottles that were sitting on the bar top. How did you get in?"

"The front entrance was open. Here, let me help you." Shane extended his hand and pulled her to her feet. "Are you okay?" He scanned the length of her to make sure she didn't have any visible cuts.

"What are you doing here?" Oh, yes. She was mad at him all right.

"I saw the lights were still on, and I wanted to talk to you about the silent auction donations we're supposed to—"

The look on her face had him stopping midsentence.

"What's wrong?" Maybe she'd been injured after all? "Are you sure you're not hurt?"

"Not hurt." She shook her head and looked away. "Letter…"

Shane couldn't understand. "What are you talking about?"

She turned to face him. Her distraught expression stole the breath from him. "Close down… Lose everything."

She wasn't making any sense. Maybe he should leave and come back another time.

A single tear fell from the corner of her eye. "What am I going to do?"

Her vulnerability tugged at his heart. "Come on. Let's go sit down, and you can tell me what's going on."

He walked to the closest table and Layla sat.

"Would you like a glass of water?" he asked.

She scrubbed her hands over her face. "Y-yes, please."

"Okay. I'll be right back." He stepped behind the bar. Shane picked up one of the broken bottles. He let out a low whistle when he read the label. *Château Lafite Rothschild Pauillac.* A bottle went for six hundred dollars, maybe more. He couldn't imagine anyone in New Suffolk spending that kind of money on a bottle of wine with dinner. The wealthy tourists who summered in their quaint little beach town, maybe, but the locals who catered to those vacationers… Most couldn't afford such luxuries, especially during the slow season.

Shane tossed the bottles in the trash. He'd help her clean up the rest of the mess later. It was the least he could do, considering he'd been somewhat responsible for creating it. *First things first.* Grabbing a glass from the shelf, he filled it with water and returned to the table. "Here you go."

"Thanks." Her large watery eyes gazed at him. Layla sipped from the glass and set it back down on the table.

"Now tell me what's got you so upset." Shane sat in the seat across from her.

She blew out a breath and recounted the story.

Shane stared at her wide-eyed. "Most banks give you more than thirty days before they make you liquidate your collateral."

Layla nodded. "I used a private lender my sister, Zara, was acquainted with."

Sounded more like a loan shark to him. *Wait.* Thirty days would put them at the end of the first week of April. "What about the gala?"

"We'll have to cancel." Tears welled in her eyes again.

"No way." The EMS department was counting on the funds this event would raise. He was counting on the money to ensure he'd keep his job. "We've sold almost all the tickets, and it's too late to find another comparable venue."

"What do you want me to do?" Layla jumped down from the chair and started pacing back and forth across the room. "We don't have the money needed to make the loan current."

"I can help you." The words erupted from him before his brain could engage.

"How?" She stopped walking midstride and turned to face him.

Shane expelled a resigned sigh. It was either help her or risk getting cut from the EMS team. "Former business investment consultant here. I can review your finances and make some recommendations on how you can make more money." Eliminating the purchase of six-hundred-dollar bottles of wine came to mind for starters.

She studied him, a hopeful glint in her gaze. "You would do that for me?"

"Yes. You have enough for the March payment, right?"

"I'll make sure of it." A tentative smile formed on her face.

"Great. We'll find a way to keep your restaurant open." At least he'd try to make that happen.

Layla walked back to the table and sat in the seat she'd vacated moments ago. "Why would you want to do this? What's in it for you?"

He wouldn't pull any punches with her. "We both know the EMS department needs the money the gala will generate. I want to make sure it happens. It's a win-win for both of us. So, what do you say?"

"Okay." Layla extended her hand to him and he shook it. Sparks of electricity sizzled through him the moment his palm touched hers.

He jerked his hand away and shoved it in his jeans pocket. What had he gotten himself into?

Layla pulled her car into the driveway of the 1930s Cape-Cod-style home on Monday evening and peered around. Strategically placed spotlights brightened the sweeping snow-blanketed front lawn. She imagined what it would look like in spring, the beds of bright fragrant blooms in a multitude of species with green Hosta and tall beach grass intermixed.

The calming ebb and flow of the ocean waves crashing on shore filled her Mini Cooper, even with the windows closed. She took several deep breaths, willing herself to stay calm.

Layla grabbed her purse and the thermal take-out bags from the passenger seat and exited the car. She walked up the blue stone walkway and rang the doorbell.

Minutes passed and no one answered the door. Had Shane forgotten he'd told her to stop by tonight? They hadn't spoken over the weekend. She should have texted him this afternoon and confirmed. She turned and started back down the walkway to her car. The snick of the lock had her stopping. She whirled around.

The door opened.

Shane appeared wearing a pair of black sweatpants slung low on his hips and... Oh, dear Lord, nothing else. No socks, no shoes. No shirt. Holy moly. She swallowed. *Perfection personified.*

"What are you doing here?" he asked.

Yes. He'd forgotten, all right. Layla cleared her throat. "You asked me to stop by tonight and bring the restaurant financial information with me. Remember?"

"Right." He nodded. "Come on in." Shane stepped aside and gestured for her to enter. "Sorry, I just got off shift and was in the shower." He shrugged into the sweatshirt she hadn't noticed in his hand.

Layla stepped inside. "Oh, my gosh. This is an amazing home." She could see through to the opposite side of the house where floor-to-ceiling windows and sliding glass doors lined the outside wall.

His gaze narrowed and every bone in his body stiffened. "It might not be much now, but wait until the renovations I have planned are complete."

"No, no." Layla shook her head. "I wasn't being sarcastic. This place is gorgeous. You must have an amazing view of the ocean from every room in the house."

He stared at her, a curious expression on his face. "Sorry. I guess I'm a little sensitive when it comes to this place. Like I said, it needs work. And yes, the views are stunning. They're what sold me on the place. The rest I can fix."

"You're doing the work yourself?" At his puzzled expression she added, "Right. Of course you are." How could she have forgotten? TK Construction had renovated her grandparents' apartment. It was where she'd met him all those years ago. Where she'd experienced her first real crush. Oh, who was she kidding? She'd fallen head over heels for him, but how could she compete with all of those Bay Beach Club teenage beauties who flirted relentlessly with him when she couldn't master the art of speech in his presence?

At least she'd finally conquered that particular phobia—funny how the threat of losing everything that mattered to you gave you something else to focus on.

She had bigger problems to worry about than making a fool of herself in front of him.

That's what she'd always been afraid of, but it didn't matter anymore.

"Want a quick tour before we get started?" he asked.

Her eyes widened. She wouldn't have expected him to offer such a thing, to be so…friendly. He'd made it clear from the start he was only helping her because it benefited the EMS department. "A win-win," he'd said. That was fine with her. She expected nothing more. Still, her curiosity got the better of her. She couldn't resist now that he'd offered. "Yes. I'd love to hear what you have planned for each room."

"Follow me." Shane walked past the staircase on the right and moved into the interior.

Layla stood in the center of the home and peered around. A large kitchen sat on the right in front of the staircase and a gigantic living room with a wide fireplace on the left. "Oh, wow. I love how all the spaces are open to each other and the view you have… spectacular."

"It wasn't that way when I bought the place. Each room was separate."

"You've done an amazing job making it so open." She wondered why he'd decided to pursue careers in finance and medicine when he obviously possessed the skill and talent to excel at the kind of work his family had been doing for years.

"I'm going to add an island in the kitchen."

"I can picture it there. In front of the dining table." She pointed to the open floor space in front of where the wall of cabinets stood. "A long, wide one with lots of counter space." The perfect place for preparing a meal.

Shane smiled and nodded. "That's exactly what I'm thinking."

She turned toward the living room. "What will you do in here?"

"I'll rip out the nasty carpet. There's hardwood underneath that matches the rest of the flooring on this level."

"Sounds perfect. All you need is a comfy sectional in front of the fireplace and a huge TV over the mantel and you're all set."

"You're reading my mind." Shane stared at her, a stunned expression on his face. "There's not much else to see on this level. We'll work at the table." He turned toward the fridge.

"Wait, please." She placed a hand on his arm to stop him.

He faced her. "What is it?"

"I just wanted to thank you again for helping me. My restaurant is…" She hesitated. How could she explain what La Cabane de La Mer meant to her? "It's more than just a job. Cooking is a part of who I am. To be able to do that on my own terms… It's a dream come true."

He studied her for long intense moments before saying, "I'm glad to help. Go ahead and grab a seat." Shane pointed over his shoulder in the vicinity of the table. "Want something to drink?"

"Actually, I brought you dinner and a bottle of red

wine. I figured it's the least I could do." Layla handed him one of the thermal takeout bags and pulled a wine bottle from her purse.

His mouth gaped. "You did?"

Layla beamed a tentative smile. "You mentioned you had to work until six. I figured you wouldn't have much time to eat before we got started, so I thought we could eat while we worked."

"Thanks." A puzzled expression crossed his face. "Where's your meal?"

"Right here." She held up a second bag.

"What'd you bring?" Shane jiggled the bag in his hand.

"Burgers. I hope you don't mind." She'd been in the mood for one. Sometimes you just got a craving for something greasy.

His eyes widened, and was that excitement in his astonished gaze? "Are you kidding? I love burgers."

Layla laughed. "Looks like we've got something in common because I love them, too."

"Thanks again for bringing this." Shane went straight for the table and sat. He unzipped the warming bag and slid the clear container from the bag. "It looks amazing."

"I stuffed the meat with Gaperon cheese and we had extra brioche rolls this evening."

"You made it?" Shane yanked the lid off one-handed. He stared at the burger as if he'd found the holy grail.

"Of course I did. Like I'd serve you fast food from—" She stopped midsentence when he grabbed the burger and took a bite.

"Oh my God." His eyes closed for a moment and a

look of ecstasy crossed his handsome face. "It *is* delicious. You're an amazing cook."

A rush of warmth flooded through her. "Thanks."

"Is this on your menu? If not, you should add it." Shane bit into the burger again.

Was he kidding? Of course he was. She owned a gourmet French restaurant, for goodness' sake. "Right." Layla grinned.

"This is really fantastic."

Layla gawked as he consumed the rest of the burger in one bite.

"Sorry." His cheeks flamed bright red. "I, ah… missed lunch and dinner." He lifted a napkin from the holder perched in the center of the table and dragged it across his mouth.

"Why did you miss lunch and dinner?"

His blue eyes sparkled and…he looked like a kid at Christmas.

"I became a godfather today." A wide happy grin spread across his face.

"A godfather?" She frowned. "Did someone have a baby?"

"Yes." His smile grew brighter and his eyes… Holy cow. They danced with delight. "I delivered my first baby this evening," he added at her confused expression.

Work. Of course. "What happened?"

"Woman was alone at home and in labor. She couldn't reach her husband and called 9-1-1." Shane grabbed a fry from the container and munched. "She was one hundred percent dilated when we arrived. No time to get her to the hospital so we delivered the baby at her home. I'm happy to say mother and son are doing great."

He'd brought a new life into this world. Helped someone when they couldn't help themselves. "That's incredible." Now she understood why he'd chosen this profession. He loved his work.

"It really is." His look of wonder made her smile.

Amazing home renovator, successful Wall Street career, EMT extraordinaire, lover of burgers. Let's not forget those fabulous abs and biceps. So many layers to this complicated man. What else made him tick? Layla wanted to know.

"The parents made me an honorary godfather."

She grinned. "Congratulations."

"Thanks." Shane stood and walked to the fridge on the far side of the room. He returned a moment later carrying a bottle of ketchup.

"Oh, you don't need that. There's some in the bag."

He set the bottle on the table and lifted the small cup filled with the dipping sauce she'd included. "This doesn't look like ketchup." He tilted the plastic cup for her inspection.

"That's the honey mustard mayo. The curry ketchup is in the other container."

"Curry ketchup?" He shot her a dubious look.

"It's good. Trust me."

Shane dipped a fry and stuck it in his mouth. His eyes opened wide and a look of surprise crossed his face. "You're right. I thought it sounded a little weird to mix curry and ketchup, but this is great."

"I'm glad you like it." She grinned.

"Okay." He licked the salt from his fingers, grabbed his laptop from the counter and brought it back to the table. "It's time to get to work. Are you ready?"

Layla reached inside her purse, withdrew the Jump-drive containing the restaurant financial records and handed it to Shane. "Let's do this."

Chapter Four

Shane lifted his coffee cup from the table and held it to his mouth. Empty. Crap. *Time to make another pot.* He rose and walked into the kitchen. Stretching his arms overhead, he tilted side to side as he waited for his caffeine infusion to finish percolating.

He gazed out the window. The first blush of dawn glinted on the horizon. What time was it anyway? The grandfather clock he and his father had made years ago chimed six times. They'd been at it all night. He had to give Layla credit; she'd stayed with him, answering his questions as he worked.

Speaking of Layla... He peered around. Where was she? Shane walked into the living room. He spotted her curled up, asleep, on the old recliner he'd set up in front of the fireplace. She'd removed the elastic that confined her hair in that austere bun she always wore, and it tumbled down in glorious waves around her face and shoulders. She looked peaceful and serene.

Shane laughed at the sight of her striped-stockinged feet peeking out from beneath her long puffy coat, which she'd used to cover herself. He shook his head. Melinda would never have been caught dead wearing anything of the sort. Not even for Halloween.

Shane studied her face, looking for a glimpse of the Layla he remembered—snobby, uptight, pretentious— No. He could knock that last word off his list. The Layla he'd brainstormed with last night wasn't fake in any way. Her sincere interest in his ideas for the house told him as much.

Was he surprised? Hell, yes. He'd expected her to scoff at him. Melinda would have. She'd never appreciated his skills and talents, except for his aptitude for making money. Now, that, she'd always valued.

Lord, how could he have been so blind?

He'd misread the situation, that's how. Melinda's interest was never in him personally, although she could've won an Oscar for her performance. Yes, she'd played the role of besotted girlfriend to perfection, and he'd fallen for it. Hook, line and sinker.

Shane chuckled to himself at the fishing reference. Dad had used the phrase all the time and he'd adopted it from an early age. Melinda hadn't even understood what he was talking about the first time he'd used it in her presence.

He'd never forget her haughty expression, or the *L* she'd made with her finger and thumb pressed against her forehead when he'd explained the reference.

He'd never used the expression again around her.
Pathetic fool.

Shane shook his head. He'd been so enthralled
with her. So ready to believe that a woman like her—
gorgeous, cultured, sophisticated—could be interested
in a small-town guy with a blue-collar upbringing that
he couldn't see the truth.

He gazed down at Layla. He wouldn't make the same
mistake twice.

Shane turned and headed back to the kitchen. He
wouldn't wake her. Not yet. Her tranquility would disappear the minute he gave her his analysis of her business.

He dragged a hand through his hair. How ironic
was it that he needed the skills from a job he'd become
disenchanted with to save the one he loved? The question was whether he could convince Layla to take his
advice and implement some of his recommendations.
She'd said she wanted to save her restaurant, but from
everything he'd seen, that meant making some signif-
icant changes. When push came to shove, would she
be willing to follow through—even if it meant making compromises?

He had. He knew all about compromising your dreams.

Shane grabbed two mugs from the cupboard and
filled them with the aromatic brew. Grasping the han-
dles, he ambled back to the living room.

Layla shifted in the chair. Her long dark lashes fluttered open. She peered around, a look of confusion on
her face.

"Morning," he said, and held out one cup.

She blinked a couple of times and her emerald gaze cleared. "Morning." Layla uncurled her legs and stood. She reached for the mug he offered. "Thanks. What time is it?"

"A little after six."

Her eyes widened and brows winged up. She shoved a swath of her long curly hair away from her face with her free hand. "Oh, my gosh. I'm sorry. I meant to close my eyes for a few minutes, not three hours."

"No worries. You answered all my questions. I finished reviewing all your financials."

Equal parts hope and dread filled her gaze. She dragged in a deep, audible breath. "And—"

His stomach jumped and jittered. Why was he nervous? He'd done this hundreds of times before. Yeah, but this time it was personal. He had a lot riding on whether or not she could turn things around in time.

Shane looked her in the eye. *Here goes nothing.* "Let's discuss my recommendations. We can sit at the table."

Layla stared at Shane trying to gauge the situation, but the expression on his face gave nothing away.

Squaring her shoulders, she sucked in a deep breath and blew it out slowly as she marched to the table. "Okay. Let's have it." She pulled out the chair and dropped down on the hard wooden seat.

Shane sat next to her. He logged in to his computer. "First off, for every day you're open you'll need to generate an extra two grand in order to come up with the money you need to cover the missed loan payments, plus late fees. That's on top of what you need in order to make the normal monthly payment due at the end of the month."

Her stomach dropped. How would she earn the extra cash in the off-season? Layla couldn't sit still. She pushed back her seat so fast the chair went airborne and crashed against the wall. "I'm so sorry." She rushed to where the chair lay on the floor. "I didn't mean to do that."

Shane beat her to the punch. He righted the chair and placed it back under the table. "It's okay. I know what I'm suggesting seems like the impossible—"

She raised her hand to stop him. The last thing she wanted was for him to patronize her. She'd had enough of that from Antoine over the years. "Layla, *ma chérie*, it's okay…" He'd said those same words every time she'd gone to him about Pierre's insubordination.

If only she'd recognized the condescending, lying, cheating bastard for what he was earlier. Maybe she wouldn't be in this situation.

Layla glared at Shane. She wouldn't allow any man to treat her like that again. "What's your plan?" She couldn't help her clipped tone.

He eyed her for a minute with an assessing glint in his gaze.

She straightened her shoulders and returned his glance with a challenging one of her own.

Shane returned his attention to his computer. "I recommend closing on Tuesdays. At least through the winter months. We can revisit that during the summer when the tourists return."

"Whoa. Wait a minute." Layla yanked out the chair and sat down next to him again. "We're already closed on Sundays and Mondays because we don't do enough business. Now you want me to close the restaurant for *three* days a week?" She shook her head. "Your plan makes no sense. How will closing generate the income we need?"

"Your operating expenses are more than you make being open. Closing on Tuesdays will save you money. That said, I'm also recommending you open for lunch Wednesday through Saturday."

Layla rubbed at her temples. First, he wanted her to close and now he wanted her to stay open longer on the days she was serving dinner. She shook her head. "But that's going to *cost* me money. I'll have to pay my kitchen and waitstaff, assuming they're all available during the day."

Shane locked his gaze on her. "That brings me to my next point. You don't need all those people on the line or the floor, especially during lunch. Two kitchen staff should be sufficient to start and a couple of servers. We can look at adding more people as your customer base increases."

Layla blanched. "What are you saying? That I have to fire people?"

He hesitated. "I'm recommending you lay off some of your staff, yes."

"No. Absolutely not." Who did this guy think he was? "Two people can't prepare the intricate meals we make. That's why I have a sous-chef and prep station cooks."

"I'm thinking lighter fare for lunch would help your overhead." He cocked his head to the side. "Like I said last night, your burger would be perfect. Maybe some sandwiches."

Her mouth fell open. She couldn't help it. *Unbelievable*. She'd believed he'd been kidding when he'd suggested she add the burger to her menu, but he wasn't. "Let me get this straight. You want me to serve burgers and sandwiches?"

"Sure. Why not? I think you can give the diner a run for their money."

He was comparing the cuisine she prepared to the local diner in town? Her hands clenched into tight fists. She might not have the Michelin star she was striving for—yet—but she was confident her restaurant could still rival most of the upscale Paris eateries.

"You'll need to change wine suppliers, too. I suggest talking to a couple of the local vineyards in the area."

That's it. Layla jumped up again and started pacing back and forth. Ordinary cuisine? Cheap wine? He was ruining her place. She marched over to where he sat and looked him in the eye. "No. I can't do that. I *won't* do that."

"Why?" he asked.

She threw her hands up in the air. "Exclusive *French* restaurant. Remember? I serve *French* wine and food to my customers."

"This is New Suffolk, Massachusetts, Layla. Not Lyon, France."

She sucked in a breath. He knew that many considered Lyon the secret foodie city in France?

"Most people who visit your restaurant can't tell the difference in flavor between your Château Lafite Rothschild Pauillac and a bottle of local wine that tastes good. What they can tell is the difference in price—and they won't order what they can't afford." He met her gaze. "How have your wine sales been lately?"

"No. You're—" She was about to say "wrong," but he wasn't. Shane was one hundred percent right. The patrons who frequented La Cabane de La Mer were nothing like the sophisticated Parisians who had dined at Antoine's bistro. This small town just didn't have the population—or the income—to sustain the same type of restaurant she'd operated in the City of Light.

Layla scrubbed her hands over her face. What was wrong with her? She didn't have to prove anything to Antoine, because that's what she'd been doing these past months. She'd wanted to show him everything he'd lost by firing her after she'd called off their marriage. She'd tried to do that by creating a bigger, better version of Chez Antoine.

And now she would be the biggest loser in this foolish game.

She swallowed hard. Her voice shook when she spoke. "Okay. I'll do it. I'll make whatever changes you suggest. This restaurant is my dream." That much hadn't changed and never would. She'd make sure she wouldn't lose out again.

"Are you sure?" Shane asked. "It's going to take a lot of hard work, and some sacrifices along the way."

Layla nodded. "I know. But I'm committed, one hundred percent. I want to save my restaurant, Shane."

"Good. I'll help you."

"Thanks. I'm going to need it. I only have one shot at getting this right." She sucked in a breath. "I have no experience creating the kind of casual food you're talking about. I'm a three-Michelin-star chef." A strangled laugh escaped from her parted lips. "Upscale gourmet is all I know."

Shane pursed his lips together. "I've got an idea. Are you busy later this morning?"

She was all ears. "No. Why?" she asked.

Shane glanced at his watch. "It's seven now. I'll pick you up at eleven at the restaurant."

"Why? I wasn't planning on going to the restaurant until much later this afternoon. We don't open for dinner until five this evening."

Shane frowned. "You don't live on the second floor of the restaurant like your grandfather did?"

"No." She explained about the lender restrictions. "I rented an apartment above the Coffee Palace."

"Got it. So, I'll pick you up there instead."

"What for? What are we doing?"

"Research." He smiled.

Research? Was he suggesting what she thought he was? Layla stared at the sexy grin plastered on his handsome face.

Was this all a pretense on his part? Review her finances, offer a few pieces of advice. What kind of payment would he expect for his services?

Her nerves felt overwhelmed—first by the emotional reality of the compromises she'd have to make. And now…this. Was Shane Kavanaugh just another man in a long line looking to undermine her confidence?

Well. She wasn't going to let it happen. She opened her mouth to give him a piece of her mind.

"Don't forget to bring your appetite." Shane winked. "There'll be lots to feast on."

Her mouth gaped. Layla slammed her hands on her hips and glared at him. "You have got to be kidding." Who did he think he was, coming on to her like that?

He stared at her as if she'd grown an extra head. "What's the big deal? I think it makes a lot of sense. We visit a few restaurants in the area and check out what's on their menus and—"

Wait. What? "Food? You're talking about…eating."

"Yeah. What'd you think I was talking about?" Shane aimed a confused expression at her.

Heat crept up her neck and flooded her cheeks.

"Oh." He seemed to understand how he'd come across. "No. I wasn't… Please don't think…" That sexy grin crossed his handsome face again.

Her pulse soared. *Have mercy.* The man was too gorgeous for his own good. "Um, don't worry about it." Her face was on fire now. She jumped up again. At least the chair stayed upright this time. "I should get going. I'll see you at eleven."

Layla raced for the door.

"Trying out French restaurants in Boston is a great idea," Layla said as he parked his truck in the public parking garage on Tremont Street.

Shane grinned. "I'm glad you agree." If she could

find a way to produce the types of dishes other popular cafés served, she'd have more of a chance at succeeding with hers. "Did you have a chance to look at all the restaurant websites I pulled up on my phone?"

"Not all of them. It was a quick drive—less than forty minutes—but I copied the links into a text and sent them to my phone. I hope you don't mind. I'll review them later."

"No problem."

"I've got lots of ideas from these." She handed him his phone. "Although, I do want to find out what the popular dishes are. To make sure I'm on the right track with what I'm thinking."

"All right. Let's get started." He shoved his phone in his jeans pocket and slipped out of the car.

They exited the garage and headed southwest on Tremont Street.

"Gosh, I can't remember the last time I came to Boston. Probably not since I was a kid. Grandpa used to visit the farmers market several times a year. He always brought me with him during the summer months when we stayed in New Suffolk. He was serving farm-to-table at his restaurant long before it became popular." Layla smiled. "I used to love accompanying him. I learned so much from him during those trips."

"Sounds like you and your grandfather are close."

"Yes." Her shoulders sagged. "He'll be devastated if I lose the restaurant. He trusted me with his most prized possession. I can't let him down."

"We're going to do everything we can to make sure that doesn't happen." That's why he'd suggested this trip. "But first, we need some inspiration for your new lunch menu." Shane stopped in front of a building with a large black awning over a wide metal-and-glass door flanked by two glass windows. "Our first stop." He opened the door and gestured for her to precede him.

Layla stepped inside and he followed. "This place makes me feel as if I've been transported to a modern Parisian bistro."

Shane peered around, taking in the wood floors and the mixture of round and square tables covered with white tablecloths. "If you say so."

Her sweet chuckle wrapped around him like a soft slip of silk. "It's more the waitstaff dressed in their pristine white shirts, black trousers and vests, and bowties than the actual decor."

"They're dressed like the servers at your place."

"Parisian bistro. My point exactly."

He still couldn't understand. He'd seen servers dressed this way in plenty of upscale restaurants in New York City. Hell, he'd worn a similar uniform all those summers he'd waited tables at the New Suffolk country club. "How did you end up in Paris, of all places? Why not Manhattan, or Boston or LA for that matter? Why go to a different country?"

"I wanted an adventure. After high school, I applied to culinary school in France. I fell in love the moment I arrived. The culture, the food and the city…" A huge smile crossed her face. The same one he'd seen the evening they'd run into each other at Donahue's and she'd told him about her restaurant.

"How come you came back?"

"My grandfather sold his restaurant to me."

Shane suspected there was more to the story. He hadn't missed the glimpse of despair in her eyes before she'd straightened and pinned a smile on her face.

The hostess appeared and escorted them to a cozy table for two with a great view of the hustle and bustle of Tremont Street. She presented a menu to Layla first, and to him. "Your server will be with you in a moment."

Layla glanced up at the hostess. "Do you have any specials this afternoon?"

"No. We don't have specials during the lunch service."

Layla nodded. "Good to know. Thank you."

"You're welcome." The hostess disappeared.

"A set list of food options makes things much easier." She opened her menu. "A few salad choices, four different sandwich selections and a couple of meat entrées. Same as the menu posted on the website."

"There's a dinner section in here, too." He glanced at the dinner selections. "Looks like the dinner menu is an expanded version of the lunch menu."

"Yes." She lifted her head and gazed at him. "I know we agreed to split a meal, but I think we should each order something different. I want to see the portion sizes."

"Sounds like a plan. What are you going to order?" he asked.

"You'll see." She flashed a smug smile.

What was that about, he wondered?

A server appeared at their table. "Bonjour. Are you ready to order?"

Layla worried her bottom lip. "I can't decide."

Huh? His brows drew together in confusion. What was she up to?

"Can you make a recommendation?" Layla asked.

"Lots of people order the chicken. It's probably our most popular dish." The waitress pointed to the dish description on the open menu Layla had set out in front of her. "But I like the veal or the salmon."

He cracked a smile. Layla had discovered the most popular dish without being obvious. She could probably give some of his old Wall Street colleagues some competition—he had to admit, that was a slick move.

"Then I'll have the salmon." Layla winked at him.

The waitress sent him a questioning glance. "What can I get for you?"

Shane thought about ordering the burger, although he doubted it would measure up to the one Layla had made for him last night. *Amazing, the woman could cook with the best of the best.* He read the veal and chicken descriptions, but neither piqued his interest. "How is the boeuf bourguignon?" Beef stew sounded good on this cold winter day, and when it came down to it, he was a meat-and-potatoes kind of man.

"Another popular dish." The waitress nodded. "It's delicious."

"I'll have that." Shane closed the menu in his hand. He collected Layla's and handed both to the server.

"Thanks." The woman turned to leave.

"So far, so good." Layla grinned. "I've got lots of

menu ideas as well as some information, and it's all thanks to you."

Shane smiled back. He couldn't help it. He liked it when she smiled. "I'm glad I could help." He meant every word.

Chapter Five

Layla stood and pushed in her chair at the head of the table. The chatter among her staff, as they ate the typical family-style meal she'd prepared for this last-minute staff meeting on Saturday afternoon, stopped and silence filled the dining room except for the sound of the waves crashing on the shore outside. "I'd like to thank you all for coming in early today. I wanted to talk to you about some changes I'm going to make here at the restaurant starting next week."

Her stomach jumped and jittered as a round of murmurs sounded around the table.

"What changes?" Sal, one of her prep cooks, laid his heavily tattooed arms across his thick chest and glared at her.

She swallowed hard as ten pairs of eyes stared at

her. "As you may have noticed, business has dropped off in the last few months."

"You're going out of business, aren't you?" Richard, another prep cook, accused.

The murmurs and watchful expressions elevated to sheer panic. Everyone spoke at once, the loud voices shrieking in her ear.

"No. No. Please. Everyone. Please settle down." Layla banged a metal serving spoon on the table in the hope the group would quiet, but the noise grew louder. Raising her voice, she shouted, "La Cabane de La Mer is *not* going out of business." She repeated her statement again for good measure.

The group finally quieted, but the silence did nothing to calm her nerves. Just the opposite. Nausea stirred in her stomach.

"What are you planning to do?" Olivia asked.

"For starters, I'm closing the restaurant on Tuesdays."

The noise erupted again before she could explain further.

"Quiet down," she commanded.

"This is bull," Sal growled. "We're already closed on Sundays and Mondays. How's a guy supposed to make a living?"

"Yeah." Richard sent her a condescending sneer. Jerking his head to Sal, he said, "Told ya so."

She couldn't catch everything Richard mumbled under his breath, but the word *bitch* came through loud and clear. Judging by Olivia's gasp, she heard the insult, too.

Layla straightened her shoulders and rose up to her

full height. All five foot, ten inches. She might not have been able to fire Pierre for the way he insulted her, but now she was the owner, and she could sure as hell take care of Richard. She wouldn't allow him to belittle her—or any other woman on her staff. "Your services are no longer needed."

Richard jumped from his seat. "What? You… Why? What did I do?"

Oh, yes. Just like Pierre. Act as if he'd done nothing wrong. "I have a zero-tolerance policy when it comes to harassment. I treat my employees with respect and I expect the same from them."

"I…I," Richard sputtered.

"I'll mail you your final paycheck." Layla pointed toward the exit. "Please leave, now."

Richard's eyes bugged out. "You've got to be kidding."

"No. I'm not."

Richard sent one final glare in her direction as he stomped across the room and disappeared.

Layla gazed around the table. "Anyone else want to leave?"

A round of *no*es ensued.

She'd always imagined she'd receive satisfaction removing people like Pierre and Richard from her kitchen; instead acid churned and burned in her stomach.

"You don't have what it takes." Antoine's words echoed in her head.

Maybe he was right after all?

The rest of the meeting passed uneventfully, although her staff was clearly a bit shaken by all the changes Shane had recommended. Still, they'd stayed with her. Made suggestions. Special pricing for seniors; a flexible work schedule to accommodate the new lunch service hours—which she'd agreed to, provided all the shifts were covered.

Yes, Antoine was wrong, all right. She had what was needed to succeed. A team.

Something Antoine was never interested in forming with his employees.

Layla lifted the industrial-size cast-iron pot from the oven and set it on the prep table.

"Hey, Layla. How are you doing?" Olivia entered the kitchen and walked over to where she stood. "You disappeared after the staff meeting and...well..."

She'd needed some time to regroup after the incident with Richard. After explaining her changes, she'd retreated to her office. "I was reviewing invoices."

"What are you making?" Olivia asked.

She removed the lid and allowed her sous-chef a quick peek.

"Ah, coq au vin. It smells fantastic. I'll finish up the other dishes for tonight."

"Okay. Sounds good." Layla set the lid down on the prep table and grabbed her phone from her pocket. She snapped a few pictures and posted the best one on the restaurant's Facebook and Instagram pages, along with the information on the new hours beginning next week and how the dish would be part of the new lunch menu.

Her phone dinged a moment later. Layla glanced at the screen. *Shane.* What could he want? There'd been radio silence from him since they'd returned from

Boston four days ago. A part of her wondered why he hadn't called to see how things were progressing. They'd begin serving lunch in a few days and she still had a lot to do. Not that she expected Shane to do any of it. He'd already given her more help than she could have imagined, but... He'd seemed invested in her success.

Lord, she prayed she could make enough money in the next few weeks to make the loan current. Layla opened the message.

That looks delicious!

Her brows furrowed as she typed her response. What looks delicious?

Her phone dinged again. She read Shane's text.

The picture of the coq au vin you just posted.

He'd followed the restaurant on social media? Why that brought a smile to her face, Layla couldn't say, but it did. Another text came through. She glanced at the screen again.

I'm salivating just looking at the picture.

She typed back, We open in two hours. Stop by. Dinner's on me. It was the least she could do.

Wish I could. I'm STARVING. She assumed he used all capital letters on the last word to emphasize his point. On shift till nine tonight. He added a frown emoji.

Layla chuckled. That could work in her favor. Her thumbs flew across the keyboard. I need a taste tester for some of the other items I want to add to the menu. Interested? I'll stick around after we close if you want to come over.

He sent her a thumbs-up emoji.

Layla grinned, a rush of warmth flooding through her. Perfect, she typed back. See you tonight.

"I'm here. Let the tasting begin," Shane announced as he strolled through the kitchen door.

Layla jumped. She whirled around, leaving the fridge wide open. "How did you get in? I locked the front door half an hour ago, after the last customer left."

"I know. I got your text. I happened to arrive as your sous-chef was leaving. She let me in and told me I'd find you in the kitchen. Didn't mean to scare you."

"Try not to sneak up on me next time," she admonished.

He let out a low chuckle. "I'll do my best. Now—" Shane rubbed his palms together "—I've been looking forward to the coq au vin all night."

Layla smiled and his heart beat a rapid tattoo. What was that all about? Yes, she had a great smile, but still…

"Do you mind eating here in the kitchen?" she asked. "My staff already set up the dining room for when we reopen on Wednesday."

He nodded, relieved to change the subject. "Not at all. Anywhere is fine."

"Okay, great. Grab that stool over there," she pointed to the far back corner. "You can slide it under the prep counter. It's clean," she added.

Shane moved to do her bidding. "Speaking of your staff, have you spoken to them yet about all of the changes you plan to make, including the layoffs?" She'd been on board a few days ago, but when push came to shove, would she follow through?

Layla walked over to the prep table and placed a small plate on the gleaming surface. She looked him in the eye. "Yes. It's taken care of."

He studied her carefully. "Are you okay? Did something happen?"

"I'm fine," Layla insisted, then shook her head. "Let's just say not everyone was happy about the modifications. It's not a problem anymore." She grabbed a set of silverware wrapped in a cloth napkin from her pocket and set it beside his plate. "I made a Niçoise salad as a starter. This is a mini version of what I'll serve for lunch. I don't want to stuff you on the first course. There's lots more to come."

He could tell she wasn't telling him everything, but he didn't press her further. Whatever had happened, the situation had obviously taken a toll on her. Whenever she talked about cooking, Layla looked…joyful. But now…some of that joy was missing.

Oddly enough, all Shane wanted to do was pull her into his arms and tell her everything was going to be all right. Which was insane considering they were practically strangers, after a decade or more of not seeing each other. So what was going on with him?

Must be the hunger talking. He swallowed hard and calmed his racing heart. Yeah, that was it.

Liar.

Layla sucked in a deep steadying breath and released it slowly. She wouldn't cry. Tears wouldn't solve anything. She'd known making changes would be a means to an end. It was just... She wished Richard could have left on better terms. His nastiness toward her had been a bitter pill to swallow.

"Oh...really, really good." Shane forked up more of the Boston lettuce, thinly sliced potatoes and tuna and lifted it to his mouth. "Definitely going to be a hit." He waggled his brows and grinned.

She laughed—she couldn't help it—and her heart seemed a little lighter. "Glad to hear it. Let me know when you're ready for your coq au vin."

"Now," he said after finishing the last bite. "Like I said, I haven't eaten since noon. I pulled another double shift today."

"Makes for a long day," she said.

"Sometimes, but I don't mind. I love what I do."

Layla smiled. "Me, too." She filled a dish with the delicious-smelling stew and placed a small piece of toasted bread on top. Grabbing some fresh parsley from a small bowl on the counter beside the stove, she sprinkled a smidge on top. "Here you go." She placed the dish in front of him. "Bon appétit."

Shane gazed at it in hunger—and a little amazement. "It looks even better than the picture."

A rush of warmth flooded through her. "Thank you. Go on. Dig in."

"What about you? Aren't you going to eat?"

"Don't mind if I do." Layla moved back to the stove and prepared another plate. When she returned, Shane had fetched another stool and placed it on the other side of the table opposite him. *Considerate.* She liked that. "Thank you, kind sir."

He smiled. "You're welcome."

She placed her dish on the gleaming metal surface and sat.

Shane lifted the fork to his mouth. He let out a groan as his lips closed around a piece of chicken. "Oh, my God. This is to die for."

She marveled at the sheer joy on Shane's face. Antoine had never taken such pleasure in anything she'd ever prepared for him. Not once in the three years they'd been together. It was only now that they'd been apart for months that she could let herself see the truth—that it had bothered her, more than she cared to admit. Cooking was an integral part of her. From the time she'd been old enough to follow her grandfather around in his kitchen. She wanted to share that part of her with someone who appreciated it.

She'd believed that person was Antoine. Had fallen head over heels for him. At least she'd believed she was in love with him. The truth was, he was her first serious relationship. She'd never had much experience with that particular emotion when it came to the opposite sex. Had he ever loved her, or were his vows of

"I can't live without you" and "you mean the world to me" just lines he spewed to get her into bed?

Face it. You suck at the whole relationship thing. Always have. Now, cooking, yeah, she excelled at that. Shane thought so, too.

"Earth to Layla. Come in, Layla."

"What?" She blinked and focused her attention on Shane.

"What were you thinking about? You seemed a million miles away."

"Wine." It was the first thing that popped into her mind as a plausible excuse, because sure as heck, Layla wouldn't make him privy to her thoughts about Antoine. No way. No how. "Would you like some?"

"That sounds great."

Good. He'd accepted her response at face value. "What would you like, white or red?" She normally paired her coq au vin with a Burgundy or a good Merlot, but Shane might prefer a Pinot Grigio.

"You choose."

"Well, the Château Lafite Rothschild Pauillac tastes delicious." Layla beamed a cheeky grin at him.

He chuckled. "A woman who can laugh at herself. I like that. But I'm thinking we should save that for a special occasion, since you only have one bottle left."

"We'll break it open when I make the loan current."

Shane grinned a heart-stopping smile. "Agreed. In the meantime—"

Layla held up a hand. "I know what you're going to ask, and no. I haven't addressed the wine situation yet. There's no rush. I just replenished the inventory last week. The good thing is that I didn't have to order any of the really expensive stock. Most of what I'd re-ordered was in the moderate range. Not the best situation, but not the worst, either."

"I was going to ask if you had some salt and pepper, but thanks for the update."

Heat crept up her neck and flooded her face. "Oh. I'll grab some from the dining room, and a bottle of wine and some glasses from the bar. Be right back." She rose and headed toward the exit.

Layla sped down the hall and into the dining room. She plucked up one salt shaker and one pepper shaker from the closest table and dropped them in her pocket. Hurrying to the bar, she grabbed an opener and uncorked a bottle of Merlot. Glasses and bottle in hands, she returned to the kitchen.

"That was quick," Shane said as she set the wine and goblets on the prep table. "I'll pour while you eat. Your food is probably getting cold by now."

Considerate and sweet. Yes, she definitely liked that. "Here are your salt and pepper." She placed the shakers in front of him. "So, how is your house coming along? Have you made any progress?" Layla forked up a portion of her meal and placed it in her mouth. Shane was right. Her food was lukewarm at best. She wasn't that hungry anyway.

Shane shook his head. "I haven't done anything since you've seen it. Tuesday was my only day off and I've been working double shifts ever since."

That explained why he hadn't been in touch. Layla frowned. Tuesday was his only day off? Instead of doing what he needed to do on his house, he'd taken her to Boston and spent the day helping her.

"I have tomorrow off. I'm planning to tackle the living room. It shouldn't take me long to patch the holes and paint. If I'm lucky, I can start on the floors."

Layla grinned. "Tomorrow is Sunday. That means the restaurant is closed. How about I come over and help you out? I can paint almost as well as I can cook."

"You want to paint my living room?"

She almost laughed out loud at the stunned expression on his face. "Sure. Why not? I know how to paint, Shane."

"You're serious?" He stared at her as if he couldn't believe it was true.

"Yes. You've done so much to help me. I want to return the favor." Not because she owed him, or because it was the least she could do. She wanted to do this.

"Okay. You're on. Come on over tomorrow afternoon. That will give me the morning to repair the walls."

Why her heart hammered a fast beat, Layla couldn't say. "I'll do that."

"Oh." Shane snapped his fingers. "There was something I wanted to talk to you about. Actually it's why I stopped by the restaurant the other night."

She'd wondered what circumstance had led to his being here. Although, now she was glad he'd come, whatever the reason. "What's that?"

"I wanted to set up a time we can get together and collect the silent auction donations."

"Oh, gosh. I'd almost forgotten about that." Layla

waved off his concern. "I can handle it on my own. You concentrate on your renovations during your free time."

Shane shook his head. "Duncan asked us to do this together. Besides, I can't imagine it will take more than a couple of hours."

"Okay. How about Tuesday at eleven? All the businesses we need to contact should be open by then. We can meet at the Coffee Palace."

"Sounds like a plan," Shane agreed. "Speaking of plans, would you mind showing me where you're planning on holding the silent auction?"

Her breath quickened. Did he not trust her to manage the gala execution? Had she been wrong about him after all?

Red color flooded his cheeks. "Honestly, I just want to see this place. I've been curious about what the rest of the place looked like since I was a kid. Dad wouldn't allow me to snoop around when TK did the upstairs renovation for your grandparents."

No more second-guessing herself. Shane was a good guy. He wasn't anything like Pierre or Richard or any of the other jerks she'd run into over the years who thought women couldn't handle responsibility in the business world.

"So, ready to start the tour?"

He smiled fully now, and the look sent a jolt through her body. "Absolutely."

Layla grinned. She couldn't help it. "Okay. Let me go and grab my keys. I'll be right back." She strode to her office. Reaching inside her purse, she grabbed her key ring and dropped it in her pocket as she headed back to the kitchen. "All right. Let's go." Layla walked toward the storage room.

"We're going to use the back staircase?" Shane sounded a little disappointed.

"Yes. This is how you accessed the upstairs during the renovations TK did all those years ago, right?"

Shane nodded. "The main staircase was off-limits."

"Not tonight, but we'll start with what's familiar." Layla flicked on the switch on the stairwell wall and climbed the steps. She flicked another switch when they reached the landing at the top.

"I don't remember there being a door here all those years ago."

Layla fished her keys from her pocket and thrust the key in the lock. "It was here, but Gramps had removed it when the TK crew was working to give them easier access." She pushed the door open. "Please." Layla stepped aside and gestured for Shane to enter.

He stepped into the hall. "If I remember correctly, that's a storage closet," he pointed to the first door directly across from where they stood. "And that's the master bedroom."

"Not quite." Layla grinned and opened the first door.

"What— An elevator?"

Layla chuckled. "Yes, although to be fair, it wasn't here when you were here working. Gramps installed it about ten years ago when my Nonny's knees started giving her trouble."

Shane closed the door and opened it again. "I would never have imagined this was here."

"My grandparents wanted to make sure they kept the integrity of the house so they removed the storage closets up here and downstairs."

"Way cool." Shane stared into the empty car. He looked like a kid who'd been turned loose in a candy store.

"Should we keep going?" she asked.

He jerked his attention to her. "Yes. Of course."

"My grandparents' room hasn't changed since you were here last, except they removed all the furniture when they moved to Florida."

"We can skip that. How about the rooms Levi and I worked on?"

"This way." She walked to the end of the hall.

Shane stopped short. "Whoa. The kitchen is opened up to the living room now."

"Yes. That happened around the same time as the elevator. TK did the work. Actually, your friend Levi was part of that change."

"Did you make chocolate-chip cookies like you did when we were here the first time?"

"You remember that?" She would never have guessed he'd remember something as insignificant. She'd never forget meeting him for the first time, but he'd seemed oblivious to her.

Shane laid a hand over his heart. "A man doesn't forget the best chocolate-chip cookies he's ever tasted."

"You liked the cookies I made that day?" Heat scorched her cheeks. "I thought you were just being nice."

"Swear to God. Best chocolate-chip cookies I've

ever tasted. Maybe you'd consider making them again sometime?" A winsome smile crossed his face.

Heat crept up her neck and flooded her cheeks. The man was too handsome for his own good. "Maybe."

"Good." Shane walked into the center of the living room. "You know, it's really a shame you can't rent this space. There's so much square footage, and it's sitting here empty."

"Oh, my gosh." She walked toward him. "You're brilliant."

"I am?" He straightened his shoulders. "How so?"

"No one can live here, but I might be able to rent the space out to another business." Layla smacked her hand to her forehead. "I can't believe I never thought of this before. I'll have my attorney review the contract I have with the private lender and check if it's possible."

Shane nodded. "Yeah. I like it."

"Me, too. Come on." She jerked her head toward the door that led downstairs. "I'll show you the rest of this place." Turning, she grabbed the key ring from her pocket and strode toward the front entrance of the apartment.

She expected Shane to follow her. He didn't move. She crashed into him. Every inch of his lean hard body touched hers.

Oh, my. Heaven on earth.

Their gazes connected and there it was, again. The all-encompassing need she'd felt the morning she'd seen him standing in the gazebo on the beach. But this burned stronger, hotter. The flames threatened to consume her.

Her knees went week.

"Whoa, are you okay?" Shane's arms clamped around her and pulled her in close.

Yes. She was more than okay. She was fantastic. "I'm fine, really."

Shane jerked away from her.

Her heart sank faster than a lead balloon.

What was he thinking, holding her so close? He'd grabbed her to keep her from falling, but when her curves pressed against him, his brain...melted down while other parts of his anatomy went on high alert. Hell, he wasn't some randy teenager anymore, even if his body would prove otherwise upon closer inspection.

Shane put some much-needed distance between them.

"Is something wrong?" Layla stared at him as if he were deluded.

She wasn't far off. "Everything is fine. I, ah—" He noticed her keys on the ground. "You dropped these." Shane bent and grabbed the ring. He straightened and held it in front of her. It was then he noticed the key chain attached. He ran his thumb over the simple copper penny hanging from a short silver chain.

"That's my lucky penny." Layla grabbed her keys from him. "It's brought me lots of good fortune over the years."

"Where did you get it?" he asked.

"It was a present. For my fourteenth birthday." She beamed a wide smile. "My secret admirer gave it to me."

"Oh, yeah? Who's your secret admirer?"

She gave him a dreamy smile. "I have no idea."

"You kept it, even though you don't know who gave it to you. Why?"

She grasped the penny and presented it to him. "This penny was minted the year I was born. That means someone took the time and made an effort to make something personal for me."

Yes. He had, but he'd been too chicken to sign his name on the card. With all the high-priced gifts she'd received, he'd been afraid she'd laugh at his handmade present.

A happy grin crossed her face and stole the breath from him. "I love it."

She loved it. He'd been dead wrong.

Chapter Six

Layla drove the short distance from her apartment to the community center on Sunday morning and parked in one of the free spaces near the skating rink. She hopped out of the car and strode toward the pavilion entrance, following the others heading that way.

"Hey, Layla," someone called on her right.

She turned and waved to the woman standing beside a red Honda Pilot a few feet away. "Hi, Mia." Layla walked over to Mia's car. "What are you doing here?"

"I signed my two youngest up to play hockey this session. What about you?" Mia's brows furrowed.

"My sous-chef's son plays, and La Cabane de La Mer donated the shirts for his team—the Lucky Pucks. Their first game is this morning. I decided to come and cheer them on."

"Looks like we're cheering for the same team."

Mia opened the passenger door of her SUV. Two girls jumped out of the car wearing Lucky Pucks shirts. "Do you remember Brooke—" Mia pointed to the taller of the two girls "—and Kiera?"

"Yes. I do. It's nice to see you again, girls."

Brooke glanced at her mother. "She owns the fancy restaurant in town that you like, right?"

"Oh, yeah," Kiera added. "We keep asking Mom to take us there, but she says we wouldn't like the food."

"I meant… It's just…" Mia groaned. "Your food is delicious, but my kids…"

Layla smiled. "Aren't used to French cooking."

"Yes. That's right." Mia blew out a breath. "They like chicken nuggets and pizza."

"Don't forget grilled cheese," Brooke added. "That's my favorite."

She'd never considered adding kids' meals to the La Cabane de La Mer menu before, but if she made her selections family friendly… It would open up a whole new customer base. "What if I added ham to a grilled cheese?" She'd already planned to add a croque monsieur to her lunch menu. It would be easy enough to include it on a dinner menu for kids, although she wouldn't call it by the French name. She'd keep it simple. Grilled ham and cheese.

"Yeah," Brooke cheered.

Layla grinned. "What other foods do you like?"

"Peanut butter and jelly sandwiches are good," Kiera said.

"Oh, yes." Layla nodded her agreement. "That's another excellent choice."

Brooke peered up at her mother. "Layla's restaurant has everything we like, so can we go?"

"We'll see." Mia shut the car door. Turning back to Layla, she said, "I've got to get these guys inside. Will you save me a seat?"

"You got it. Good luck, girls." She headed toward the right side of the rink, opposite the team boxes, and found a free spot on the bench in the third row.

Layla pulled out her phone and scanned through Facebook posts while she waited. She wasn't sure how much time had passed when Mia appeared.

"Hi." Mia heaved out a sigh and dropped down beside her.

"How's it going?" Layla asked.

"It's good." Mia smiled and waved at one of her daughters. She turned her attention back to Layla. "The girls are so excited to play. It's really nice of you to come down here and watch when I'm sure you have better things to do with your day."

Layla waved off the notion. "The restaurant is closed and I don't have any plans until later this afternoon."

"Doing anything fun?" Mia let loose a disparaging chuckle. "I'm on mom duty twenty-four-seven these days so I like to live vicariously through my single friends."

Layla grinned. "Afraid not. Painting is on my agenda. I'm helping…" She was about to say Shane, but stopped herself, although she wasn't sure why. "A friend."

"Lucky friend," Mia said. Her phone dinged. She glanced down at the screen. Her expression turned grim.

"Are you…okay?" Layla asked.

Mia gave a small smile. "Yeah. My soon-to-be ex-husband just texted me. He was supposed to take the girls this afternoon, but he can't."

"I didn't realize you and your husband split."

"It's still pretty new." Mia dragged a hand through her hair. "Kyle moved out about three months ago."

Layla gasped. "I'm so sorry."

Mia shook her head. "As if his leaving wasn't stressful enough, he's been traveling for work. A lot. He's leaving on another business trip this afternoon." She couldn't hide her frustration. "Needless to say, things are a bit crazy these days. I'm just fortunate I've got my mom. She's been such a big help with the girls. Shane, too."

"Shane, as in your brother?" Layla's jaw dropped.

"I know." Mia nodded. "He's great with the girls. A real natural. He took care of them for a couple of months, before he got his EMT job. Without Shane, and my mom, I wouldn't be finishing up my teaching certificate, and I wouldn't have landed a job as one of the first grade teachers at the elementary school in the fall."

She shouldn't be surprised. Of course the man who'd volunteered to help her save her restaurant, who took the time to drive her to Boston for a day of research for her new lunch menu would help his family when they needed him.

Was Shane Kavanaugh too good to be true?

Shane finished sanding the last living room wall. Cutting the power, he climbed down from the scaffolding and set the electric sander aside. He peered around the space. Yes. The room was coming together nicely. Soon he'd have a roaring fire in the fireplace and a game on the large flat screen he planned to hang above the mantle. He'd buy a plush sectional couch with recliners so he could relax at the end of a long day.

The doorbell chimed.

"Hang on a second. I'll be right there." Shane wiped his hands on the back of his jeans to clean off the dust as he strode toward the front entrance. He opened the door. "Can I help—" His mouth dropped open. Layla stood before him, her long hair thrown up in a haphazard bun on the top of her head, dressed in a pair of black yoga pants that fit her lean hips to perfection. He spotted a cropped baggy gray sweatshirt under her open parka. She looked...sexy as all get-out.

"Hey." Layla aimed a tentative smile at him. "Is now a good time?" She glanced at her watch. "It's after noon."

"What are you talking about?"

"Are you ready to start painting?"

His mouth fell open. Okay yes. She'd told him she was serious about helping him yesterday, but he hadn't believed her. He'd never pictured... Melinda and her friends would never have...

No. Layla wasn't anything like Melinda or her friends. She was kind and thoughtful. This was the woman who'd kept a homemade gift from a stranger because someone took the time to make it for her. "No, you got it right." He grinned. "Come on in." He moved aside to allow her entry.

Layla picked up an orange five-gallon bucket that stood by her feet and stepped inside. One that had been used for painting before if the rainbow of colors dotting the exterior were anything to go by.

"What's in there?" he asked.

"Mostly rags. Some miscellaneous painting supplies, too. I wasn't sure what you'd have so I brought my own stuff. Just in case."

He appreciated her preparedness. "I have enough supplies for you to use, too."

Once in the foyer, Layla set down the bucket and shrugged off her coat.

"Let me take that for you." Shane grasped the parka and hung it in the hall closet.

"Thanks. So where should I start?"

"My, aren't you eager." He liked that about her. Once she set her mind to something, she marched forward—full steam ahead.

Hand on hip, she pulled a face. "I didn't come here to chitchat. I came to paint. I know what I'm doing. I'm the one who repainted the restaurant."

"You?" He thought she'd hired someone.

"Yes. It was much cheaper than paying a professional to do it." She peered up at him. "I know you think I'm a financially irresponsible prima donna who has no idea what it takes to run a business, but I'm not totally incompetent. I got a little lost, but I'm back on track and determined to make my place a huge success."

Shane nodded. "I agree. That's why you've decided to add a kids' menu—right?"

She gawked at him. "How did you know about that?"

"Mia and the girls stopped by earlier. Kiera told me all about how they were going to have lunch at your restaurant someday soon."

Layla gave a tentative smile. "I thought a more family friendly place would draw in new customers."

What was it about her smile that sent his heart racing? "You're right, especially when our tourism picks up again in the summer months." Shane winked. "Way to go."

She rolled her eyes and let out a sweet-sounding laugh. "It's time to start painting."

"Yeah, we've only got a few hours."

"Do you have plans tonight?" she asked.

Shane nodded. "The guys are coming over. We're gonna have a few beers and watch the game."

"Where?" She gestured around the space. "This room is empty and I doubt the paint will dry by the time your friends arrive."

"You're right. That's why I dragged the old sofa and recliner that used to be in here into the dining room." The space was big enough to accommodate the extra furniture. "I'll bring down the big TV from my bedroom and set it on the table later."

"Sounds like you've got it all worked out." Layla gave him a thumbs-up.

"What about you? I hear you're hanging with the girls. I hope you enjoy your chocolate fest."

She let out a snort. "Ah, Mia must have told you we play cards for chocolate, not cash."

He nodded. "Why you'd want to do that is beyond me."

"It gives us something to eat while *we're* watching the game." She picked up her bucket and strode into the living room.

His eyes rounded and he hurried after her. "You like watching hockey?" Melinda had hated his ritual of getting together with friends to watch the game.

"Heck, yes. Especially this time of year. I can't wait to see which teams will advance in the playoffs."

"You're just one surprise after another," Shane said.

"I'll take that as a compliment." She threw a cheeky grin at him.

"That's how I meant it."

A pink flush rose up the column of her elegant neck and flooded her cheeks. "Enough chitchatting. Let's get to work."

"Yes, ma'am." He straightened and gave her a mock salute. "Use the light gray paint on the walls, white on the trim." He pointed to the two cans sitting to the right of the fireplace. "We'll have to wash down the walls first to remove the dust since I just finished sanding. I'll get some water. Be right back."

Shane hurried into the kitchen and grabbed two square buckets from the pantry. He tossed a clean sponge in each and filled them with warm water. Grasping one handle in each hand, he returned to the living room, careful not to spill any of the water as he made his way.

He placed one pail at the end of the room nearest the kitchen and brought the other to the opposite end of the long room, at the front of the house. "You start here. We'll work our way around the room and meet in the middle."

"Okay. Mind if I put on some music while we work?" Layla pulled her cell from her pocket.

Shane shrugged. "Sure. Why not?"

"What kind of music do you like?" she asked.

"Pretty much everything. Except… Opera isn't exactly my thing. And no elevator music, either."

"Not to worry. I'm not a huge fan of either myself. I have a playlist that has a good mix of oldies, pop and rock."

"Sounds good." He walked back to his end of the room. Grabbing the wet sponge from the bucket, he wiped the dust from the wall.

The music started. "One Week" by the Barenaked Ladies blared from the speakers. Shane smiled. Yes, Layla Williams was one good surprise after another.

Layla dipped her roller in the paint. A few more touch-ups and she'd be done.

"Want a drink?"

She whirled around. Shane stood a foot away, his arm outstretched as he offered her a bottle of water. Paint splattered across his face and sweatshirt. The same color she'd just dipped her roller in. "Oh, my gosh." Her mouth dropped open. "I'm so sorry. You startled me."

Shane stood stiff as a board for a moment. He leaned over and set the water bottle on the floor. Rising, he pulled one cuff of his sweatshirt into his hands and dragged the material across his face. He blinked a couple of times and drew in an audible breath. "You've been working hard for the last two hours. I thought you might be thirsty."

She glanced from the bottle of water on the floor to him. He didn't look happy. Crap. Layla flashed what she hoped was an appreciative smile. "That was very thoughtful." She set the roller in the pan and reached for the bottle, taking a long drink. "Thanks," she added after putting it back down.

"You're welcome."

She noticed a splotch on his neck as he spun away. "Oh, you missed a spot. Here, let me get it for you." Layla reached into her bucket and grabbed one of the rags.

Shane faced her again. "Don't worry about it. Wouldn't want to stain your nice shirt there."

Layla glanced down. She held Antoine's old button-down dress shirt in her hand. It was one of a few pieces of his clothing that had ended up with her things, somehow. Her hand clenched around the fabric.

He'd had the gall to ask for the items back when he realized they were missing.

Jerk.

Fat chance that was going to happen after the way he'd treated her.

She thought about pitching his things, but decided to keep them. Antoine would hate the fact that she'd turned his expensive custom-made clothes into paint rags. She grinned. "This old thing? Don't worry about it."

"I'm fine." Shane strode back to his side of the room. She started working again.

"Layla?" he called a moment later.

She turned to face him. "What?"

Shane stood close to her. His wet paintbrush and the I'm-going-to-get-you grin told her exactly what he planned to do.

Roller in hand, she squared her shoulders. "You wouldn't dare."

"Oh, yes I would."

Before she could jump out of reach, he extended his arm and painted a wide stripe down the front of her sweatshirt. Her eyes widened; mouth gaped. Moving fast, she dragged the roller down his right sleeve and smirked in satisfaction.

Shane arched a brow. He glanced down his nose at the stripe of light gray paint on his sleeve, then returned his attention to her.

She caught the mischief in his gaze. "No way." She took off toward the front entry, laughing so hard she thought she might fall over.

Shane's deep rumbly chuckle told her he was in hot pursuit.

"I'm sorry." She glanced over her shoulder. "It was an accident."

"I don't think so."

She danced out of reach when he tried to grab her. Layla raced through the arch in the entryway that led to the kitchen. He couldn't catch her, but the featherlight touch of his brush told her he'd streaked paint across the back of her neck. She shrieked with laughter and kept moving toward the dining area.

All of a sudden, Shane stood in front of her, that

cocky grin of his plastered across his face. He must have doubled back through the entryway and into the living room, which was connected to the dining space, and come at her from the opposite direction. The surprise move caught her off guard. He'd trapped her between him and the table.

She stopped short. "Stay back." She waved the roller in front of her, hoping it might scare him off.

"Not a chance. You, Ms. Williams, are going to pay." He stalked toward her.

Layla set a hand on her hip. "It's your own fault, you know."

"How's that?" he asked conversationally, taking another step closer.

She backed up and hit the table. He invaded her space. Layla laughed. She leaned back to create some distance between her and the paintbrush he held close to her face. Her eyes widened as he lowered the brush toward her cheek. His large body loomed over her. The scent of musk filled her nostrils. She breathed a lungful of air. He smelled good. Really good.

Oh, my. Layla almost groaned out loud.

Something flickered in his gaze. An emotion she'd never seen before. Strong and deep, it pulsed between them.

"Well?" His minty breath tickled her cheek. "Why am I to blame?"

Layla stared into his gorgeous blue eyes. Whatever she'd seen earlier had disappeared, or maybe she'd just imagined the whole thing. "I've…" She swallowed hard and cleared her throat. "Told you before not to sneak up on me."

Shane let out a deep belly laugh and backed away.

Relieved, she relaxed and stopped trying to analyze things.

"Yes, you have. I'll have to remember that in the future."

"You'd better." She straightened up and tugged down her sweatshirt.

Armed with his brush, he stepped closer. "What was that?" he asked, his voice low and gravelly. "I didn't catch what you said." His lips curved into a wicked grin.

Laughter bubbled up inside her. "Nothing." She shook her head. "I didn't say a word."

"That's what I thought." He lowered his hand and placed some space between them. A lopsided smile curved his lips. "Thanks for all your help today. We got a lot done."

"My pleasure." It was true. Layla couldn't remember the last time she'd had this much fun. "I'm happy to help you again, if you need me."

"I might take you up on that offer."

Layla hoped he would.

"I should clean up." Shane backed up a few steps, but didn't turn his gaze from her.

"I'll help you," she blurted.

"Don't worry about it." He aimed that smile she loved so much at her again, and her heart beat a rapid rhythm. "You've got a card game to prepare for."

"I've got plenty of time." Layla waved off his concern.

"Thanks. I appreciate the help." Shane gestured for her to proceed him.

She poured the paint in her pan back into the gallon can and capped it. Moving to the sink, she washed the remaining paint residue from her hands. She grabbed a towel. Turning, she propped herself against the counter and dried her hands. "Oh, wow." Layla glanced out the wall of windows overlooking the ocean. "Look at that." Bands of red, orange and purple streaked the early evening sky.

Shane stepped up beside her. "Beautiful. If we hurry, we can watch the sunset." He disappeared and returned a moment later. He held out her coat for her.

"Thanks." Layla removed her sweatshirt carefully. "Wouldn't want to get any wet paint on this." She slid her arms through the sleeves and zipped up.

"Nope." Shane laughed as he did the same and she followed him outside to the back deck. They stood in reverent silence, awed by the majestic beauty of the big, bright yellow orb of the sun as it plunged toward the horizon. They watched until the last speck of brilliant color faded to inky black and the stars twinkled in the heavens.

A light breeze blew and Layla shivered.

"I guess I didn't realize how cold it got—I was so absorbed. We should go in," Shane said.

"Yes," she agreed—a little reluctantly, despite the cold. She'd been enjoying just being with him.

"After you." Shane opened the door and stepped aside to allow her entrance.

Layla blinked and waited a beat for her eyes to adjust to the sudden brightness of the inside lights.

"That was really something." Shane shed his coat and draped it over the closest dining room chair.

"Absolutely stunning." She left her parka on, thankful for the extra warmth it provided. "I've been working nights for so long I can't remember when I've seen such a gorgeous sunset."

"Me, either." Shane moved into the kitchen. "Would you like a cup of coffee to warm up?"

Yes, yes, yes. She didn't want to leave. Not yet. The grandfather clock in the front entrance chimed five times. Hell. She needed to be at Elle's by six and still had to shower and make a contribution to the evening's nibbles. Layla sighed. "I should get going."

"I'll walk you out." He came over to where she stood.

"You don't have to do that."

"Yeah, I do." Shane shrugged into his coat again.

They walked to her car, the shimmering stars lighting their way.

"Thanks again," he said as he opened her car door.

She slipped behind the wheel and clicked her safety belt into place. "You're welcome."

"Drive safe." He gave a little wave.

Considerate, sweet, helps his family, a gentleman and concerned for her well-being. Could he be more perfect?

"I will." Layla started the engine.

His smile warmed her from the inside out. That warmth stayed with her the entire ride home.

* * *

Pot holders in hand, Layla carried the hot oval ceramic baking dish across the hall to Elle's apartment. She rang the doorbell with her elbow.

"Coming," called a voice from inside. Elle appeared in the door opening a moment later.

"Sorry I'm late." Layla presented her hors d'oeuvre. "I got a late start on making the buffalo chicken dip." She'd left Shane's later than anticipated. Lord, had they really chased each other around the house with paintbrushes?

"What are you smiling about?" Elle asked, a look of confusion on her face.

"Huh?" Layla's brows drew together.

"You said something about getting a late start and then started grinning like you'd won the lottery, or something."

"I didn't win the lottery." The thought of Shane had made her…happy. She'd enjoyed spending time with him.

"Are you going to stand there all night with that goofy grin on your face?" Elle gestured for her to enter.

"No." Layla pinned what she hoped was a neutral expression in place. She stepped into Elle's living room. The apartment was similar to her own, with the opposite layout. The front door opened into a long narrow room. Living room, dining room, kitchen—all open to each other—but Layla's bed and bathroom stood on the opposite side of the kitchen than Elle's.

"Hi, Layla," Abby called from her seat next to Mia

on the plush gray sofa that separated the living room from the dining area.

"Hi, ladies." Layla swerved around the circular wood dining table as she made her way to the kitchen island where other hors d'oeuvres dishes sat.

"Hey, what's that on the back of your neck?" Elle asked as she followed.

"There's something there?" She twisted her head from side to side in a futile effort to see what Elle was talking about.

"Yes." Elle pointed to the spot where her shoulders met her neck.

Layla touched her hand to the spot Elle indicated. "I don't feel anything."

Elle plucked Layla's hand away and scrutinized the area further. "It's light gray paint. You must have brushed up against a wet surface."

"What's with the light gray paint these days?" Mia asked. "I don't get it."

"It's a trendy color," Abby said.

"I know. Shane picked it for his living room." Mia shook her head. "What I want to know is why. It seems cold to me. Personally, I like warm colors. Wait." She turned her gaze to Layla. "You were over at Shane's today. That's the painting you mentioned doing when I saw you this morning, at the skating rink."

Busted. Heat invaded her cheeks. "Um." Why hadn't she told Mia she was going to help Shane, instead of being vague? It was not as if she'd done anything wrong. Now, it looked like she was trying to hide something. She squared her shoulders. "Yes. I was."

"Oh." Elle drew out the word. She joined Layla at the kitchen island and propped her elbows on top. "You're blushing like a schoolgirl. What happened?"

"Must have been good. You're redder than a fire engine." Abby's gaze glinted with amusement.

"Is there something going on between you and my brother?" Mia aimed an astonished gaze in Layla's direction.

And that's why she'd been vague. She'd wanted to avoid this question. "There's nothing between Shane and me. I mean… Well…"

"Yes?" Abby arched a brow and smirked. "You were saying?"

Layla huffed out a loud breath. "It's not what you think."

"Then what is it?" Mia let out a soft chuckle. "Because you're even redder than before."

Layla slapped her hands to her cheeks. Her face felt like it was on fire. "We're just friends."

"Right. Friends." Abby winked.

"We are," Layla insisted. "He's helping me work on getting my restaurant back on track and I—"

"What's wrong with your restaurant?" Abby asked.

Layla sighed. "Long story short, I got myself into some trouble and Shane's helping me change my business model so I can be more profitable."

"Is that why you're opening for lunch now?" Mia asked.

"That's only one of the changes he recommended. I'm still working on implementing some others."

"Is there anything we can do?" Elle asked.

Layla arched a brow and flashed a winsome smile. "Tell all your friends to come to the restaurant."

"No problem there." Abby slung an arm around her shoulder. "We've got you covered, right, girls?"

"Right," Elle and Mia answered in unison.

"Enough talk about my problems. Let's play some cards."

"Wait a minute. We can't forget this." Elle grabbed an open bottle of red wine from the counter. "Who wants some?"

"I'll have a glass." Layla released her breath, grateful for the subject change.

Elle filled the glass about halfway and handed it to her. Layla swirled the red liquid and noted the excellent bouquet. She sipped from the glass. "This is good."

"It's from a Connecticut winery. My college roommate told me about it when I visited her last month. It's a great find and a great price, too. Only twenty dollars a bottle," Elle said.

Layla picked up the bottle and glanced at the label. Brookside. She'd never heard of the vineyard. She set the bottle down on the counter. Grabbing her cell from her pocket, she snapped a picture. "This would make a great addition to my wine list." She gestured to the bottle of white wine. "Is the Pinot Grigio as good?"

"Yes. I think so." Mia held up her half-filled goblet as she walked over to where Layla and Elle stood. "It's delicious. Here." She handed the glass to Layla. "Try it."

Layla sipped from the glass and nodded. "You're right. It is really good." She handed the glass back to

Mia. *And the price is right.* Layla snapped another picture of that label, too. She couldn't wait to tell Shane about her find.

"How about you, Abby?" Elle asked.

"I'll have the Pinot." Abby rose and ambled to the table. She sat in one of the chairs and grabbed the deck of cards from the center. "Time's a wasting, and there's a lot of chocolate at stake." She shot a get-a-move-on glance at Layla, Elle and Mia.

"Yes, ma'am." Layla grabbed the seat at the table to the right of Abby.

"What are we playing?" Elle set a glass on the table in front of Abby and sat in the empty seat next to her.

"Dealer's choice," Layla called.

Abby grinned. "Blackjack is the game." She slid a fun-size bag of M&M's into the center of the table.

Mia sat in the empty seat and added her candy to Abby's. "That's the game where you try and get your card total closer to twenty-one than the dealer, without going over twenty-one, right?"

"Yes," Elle answered. She pushed her bag to the center of the table.

Layla reached into her purse and pulled out her stashes. She lined up her candies from highest value to lowest. Hershey's Nuggets, Reese's Peanut Butter Cup Miniatures and small packets of M&M's. She added her chocolate to the pile.

Abby dealt two faceup cards to each of them. To herself, she dealt one card faceup and another facedown.

Layla glanced at her cards but managed not to show

her glee. Jack of clubs and queen of hearts. The two face cards were worth ten points each.

Elle scrunched up her nose. "Hit me."

Abby placed the six of hearts next to Elle's five of diamonds and three of clubs.

"Me, too." Mia groaned when Abby tossed a king of diamonds on her queen and three of spades. "Twenty-three. I'm out."

"I'll stay," Layla said.

Abby peeked at her facedown card. She grinned and drew another from the deck.

"You've got thirteen showing." Elle gestured to Abby's cards. "I've got fourteen and Layla has twenty. I'll take another." She turned her attention to Layla. "How are things going with the spring gala?"

Abby added a three of hearts to Elle's hand. "How about you, Layla?"

"I'm good." To Elle she said, "It's all coming to-gether." Providing she could get herself out of the mess she'd created at her restaurant.

"Have you got a date yet?" Abby drew the two of spades and placed it next to her other cards.

"No. I'm going to be too busy running the kitchen," Layla answered.

"One more," Elle said when Abby held out the deck. "Phew," she added when Abby handed her the ace of clubs. She leveled her gaze on Layla. "It's been almost a year. It's time to get back out there."

"No." Layla shook her head when Abby presented the deck to her. "There's no one I'm interested in taking."

"Maybe you'll meet someone there," Mia said. "It's a regional fundraiser."

Not likely. She wasn't interested in looking for someone, either. Saving her restaurant was her priority.

"Maybe you've already met him." Abby arched a brow and flipped over another ace and laid it down in front of Elle.

Layla let out a little chuckle. "I hope you're not referring to Shane."

"There's that blush again." Elle smirked as she glanced at Layla's hand.

"There's nothing between Shane and me."

"We're just friends," Mia, Abby and Elle said in unison. They burst out laughing.

"We are. He's helping me with my restaurant and with the gala. That's all," Layla insisted, and yes, the heat radiating from her cheeks could warm the dining room at La Cabane de La Mer without lighting the fireplace.

"If you say so." Laughter flickered in Elle's gaze. "Well, I can't beat your twenty unless I take another card." She let out a loud resigned sigh. "Deal me another."

Abby handed Elle a four of diamonds. "That makes twenty-three. You're out."

Elle rolled her eyes. "You don't have to sound so cheery about it."

More laughter ensued.

"All right. Enough is enough." Layla gestured to Abby. "What have you got?"

"Sure I can't interest you in another card?" Abby

lifted the edge of her facedown card and grinned. "This is your last chance."

"No way." Layla shook her head. "Come on, stop stalling, flip it over."

Abby turned over a two of diamonds.

"That's only seventeen," Mia said.

"Son of a gun." Abby scowled and shoved the pile of candy toward Layla.

"Thank you very much." Layla gathered her bounty and grinned. "Winner deals next, and I choose five-card stud. Ante up, ladies." She tossed in four Reese's Peanut Butter Cup minis and dealt a round. Pinning a neutral expression in place, Layla peeked at her hand. Ace, king, queen, jack and ten of clubs. A royal flush. A lucky hand indeed.

Tonight was shaping up to be a great night.

"Anyone need a beverage?" Shane asked.

"I'm good for now," Duncan said.

"Me, too," Levi and his brother, Nick, said in unison.

"Okay. I'll be right back." He walked from the dining area and into his kitchen and grabbed a beer from the fridge.

The doorbell rang.

"That'll be Coop. I'll let him in," Levi said.

Shane returned to his seat on the couch. Leaning forward he plucked up another cracker and some cheese from the tray on the coffee table in front of him. "Thanks for bringing the upgraded snacks, by the way." He clapped Nick on the back.

Nick grinned. "You can thank my fiancée for that. She insisted I couldn't come over empty-handed."

"Here I was thinking this spread was standard fare." Duncan snagged some pepperoni. "But hey, what do I know since this is my first time hanging with all of you?"

"If only." Shane chuckled. "Standard fare is typically a bag of chips, a bag of pretzels or a can of peanuts." His brows drew together. "What's your fiancée's name?" He couldn't remember.

"Isabelle," Nick replied. "And don't you start in on me about how we don't know each other well enough. I get enough of that from my brother."

Shane lifted his hands in mock surrender. He agreed with Levi, but would keep his opinion to himself. At least for now. "I was going to say give Isabelle my thanks." He picked up a slider and popped it in his mouth. It was good, but couldn't hold a candle to Layla's burgers. Hers topped the charts.

Shane's phone dinged. He glanced at the screen. Layla. Had she known he'd been thinking of her? He opened the message.

She sent a picture of a huge pile of various chocolates and included the caption, I cleaned up tonight!

He texted back, Yeah you did. Congratulations. What are you going to do with all that candy?

A picture of several empty candy wrappers came through. He laughed and responded, You know, too much of that will make you sick. Fun fact—I love Reese's Peanut Butter Cups and anything Hershey, too.

I'll keep that in mind, Layla texted back and added a smiley face emoji.

"You do that," Shane muttered.

"Huh?" Cooper waved a hand in front of his face. "What are you talking about? I asked how your home renovations are going? I guess good if the living room is anything to go by."

Shane glanced at Cooper. The light blue shirt he wore reminded him of the shirt Layla held in her hand when she'd offered to clean off the paint she'd accidently flung at him earlier. A man's dress shirt, and an expensive one at that. He recognized the hand-tailored quality. He'd owned a closetful when he'd worked on Wall Street. "This old thing," she'd said when he called her on it, but he'd seen the flash of pain in her gaze before she could hide it. The same pain he'd seen when they'd had lunch in Boston a few days ago.

Another piece of the puzzle that was Layla Williams. He wanted to figure out how to fit the pieces together.

Chapter Seven

Layla rushed down the back stairs of her apartment building on Tuesday and hurried around to the front entrance of the Coffee Palace. Of all mornings to sleep through her alarm, why did it have to happen today?

She glanced at her watch as she stepped up to the counter and breathed out a sigh of relief. Five minutes to spare.

"Look who is sitting in the corner at the far side of the room." Elle pointed to her right after she greeted Layla.

Layla glanced in the direction Elle indicated. Shane sat with his back to her. She hadn't beaten him here, but she wasn't late, either. That was a good thing.

Elle cracked a smug smile. "He says to tell you where he is when you arrive."

"Okay. Thanks. We're collecting the rest of the donations for the silent auction today," she added hoping to stifle any additional remarks Elle might make.

"If you say so." Elle grinned.

"Oh, for goodness' sake." Layla rolled her eyes. She should have picked somewhere other than here to meet Shane this morning. "I'd like a coffee and an apple fritter, please," she ordered, praying her cheeks hadn't flamed bright red.

"Coming right up." Elle moved to pour her coffee. She returned with a cup and pastry a few moments later. "Have a nice day."

Layla grabbed her items and walked to the table where Shane sat. "Hi." She laid her hand on the chair top to move it out, but Shane beat her to the punch.

"Allow me." He pulled out her chair and gestured for her to have a seat.

Layla stared at him in awe. She couldn't remember the last time anyone pulled out a chair for her. Shane Kavanaugh was quite the gentleman, for sure.

"How are you this morning?" he asked when he returned to his seat.

"I'm well. Thanks. How about you?"

"Good." He shot her a quizzical glance. "Ready for tomorrow?"

Her new lunch hours would start. Would Shane's strategies pay off? *Please, please, please.* "I think so."

"Don't worry. You'll have at least one customer when you open." He beamed a devastating grin.

He'd be there. Why that turned her insides to mush, she couldn't say. Layla smiled and slipped the apple fritter from the bag. She bit into the goodness and let out a little groan of pleasure as the sugar coated her mouth.

Shane's brow winged up. "That good, huh? Care to share?"

"Don't think that boyish charm is going to work on me, mister. I'm starving." Oh, who was she kidding? Layla broke off half of the pastry and handed it to him. How could she say no to the hopeful expression on his face?

"You think I'm charming, huh?"

Charming, delightful, fun to be around, too—way more fun than Mr. Serious, Antoine—but no way would she admit that to Shane. "Don't get cocky." She couldn't help the grin that formed on her face.

He bit off a small chunk. "Oh, yeah. You're absolutely right." He licked the sugar glaze from his lips and a shiver danced down her spine.

She'd add captivating and magnetic to her list. And that mouth. What would he taste like if he kissed her? *No, no, no.* What was she thinking? "Do you know which shops we need to speak with?"

"Right here." Shane pulled out his phone. He touched the screen a couple of times and read, "Weldon's Hardware store, Rodney's auto repair, Samantha's Nail Salon and the new boutique that opened a few months ago. We can get started whenever you're ready." He popped the last piece of apple fritter she'd given him into his mouth and wiped his hands on a napkin in front of him while he chewed.

"We can go now." Layla placed the remainder of her fritter back in the white paper bag. Grabbing her coffee, she drank one last swallow and stood. "I'll take these with me and eat them on the way. We should hit the boutique first. It's the closest business to here."

"Let's do it." Shane seized his coffee and followed her to the door.

Layla's cell buzzed as they started up Main Street. "Hang on a second." She stopped and pulled the phone from her pocket. "Looks like I've got a meeting with Mark and Duncan tomorrow at five."

Shane shot her a curious glance. "A full committee meeting?"

Layla shook her head. "Just me. Mark wants to run through the timing of the food service for the gala so they can finalize the agenda for the evening."

"Are you available? Isn't that when you start serving dinner?"

"It's not a problem. My sous-chef will be handling the kitchen in the evenings starting tomorrow and I'll handle lunch. At least for now." She sent a quick note back to Duncan confirming the appointment. "Okay. Let's collect those donations."

"Wait." He pulled two envelopes from his pocket and handed them to her. "I meant to give you these at the coffee shop, but I forgot."

Layla peered inside the first and frowned. "It's a photograph of a lion and her cub."

Shane nodded. "It's a Jax Rawlins photograph. He's agreed to donate it for the silent auction."

Her eyes bugged out. She couldn't help it. "How did you get a world-famous photographer to make a donation?"

"Jax is from New Suffolk. We grew up together. I called him last week and told him it was for a good cause."

"This is amazing. It's going to bring in a ton of money."

"Maybe not a ton. This is New Suffolk, not Manhattan."

"I know a lot of Manhattan people who'd be interested in making a bid on this. It's a Jax Rawlins photo, for goodness' sake. I can't wait to see what's in here." She waved the second envelope in the air, and tore it open.

Layla found a two-hundred-dollar gift certificate to Weldon's. "You already collected the hardware store's donation?"

"No. That's my contribution."

"You purchased this to donate?" She lifted the certificate in her hand.

"Yes. I figured it's something anyone could use."

She couldn't believe it. None of the other committee members had made donations. "This is really generous of you."

"Not as generous as Jax's donation, but I wanted to do my part to support the silent auction. It is for the EMS department after all."

"Don't sell yourself short. You asked Jax to make the donation and you decided to make your own contribution. You really are a nice guy, aren't you?" *Not too good to be true after all.*

"I hope so. I try to be." The tips of his ears turned bright red.

So why was she still surprised every time? Maybe she still couldn't reconcile the man before her with the cutthroat persona she'd always associated with the Wall Street type? Hollywood movies hadn't helped and the few traders she'd met over the years only reinforced her perceptions. "Can I ask you something?" She slanted a sidelong gaze at him as they walked.

"Sure. What do you want to know?"

"How did you end up working on Wall Street? I get the whole paramedic career path, especially since you went to Hofstra University for premed, but I don't understand the connection between the two."

Shane let out a low gravelly chuckle that sent shivers skating down her spine. "My college roommate was a finance major. At the end of our sophomore year, we both got summer jobs working at his father's business investment consulting company. He identified failing businesses for investors and made recommendations on how to fix them. Turned out I had a knack for the work."

She understood. "You liked breathing new life into the companies. Making them healthy again."

"Yes. Exactly. So, I changed my major and got a business degree with a minor in finance and accounting." He shot her a curious glance. "How did you know I went to Hofstra for premed? I haven't seen you since that last summer I worked at the country club right after I graduated from high school. It's been ten years. Did my sister tell you?"

"No." *Damn.* The words were out of her mouth before she could stop them. She should have said yes and left it at that. Now he was going to want to know who had told her.

"Then how did you find out?"

Maybe she could finesse this? Layla lifted her shoulder in a casual shrug. At least she hoped it came across that way. "I've come back a few times since then to visit my grandparents." That was true. "Your name came up a time or two." *Also true.*

"Did you ask about me?" He flashed a wolfish grin.

Heat rose up her neck. "I may have." But she hadn't asked her grandparents about him. All those years she'd made a point of running into his mother to see how he was doing... Yeah, Layla would die of embarrassment if he knew the truth.

"Ah." Shane drew out the word. "Now I get it."

So, he knew. Her cheeks were on fire. Lord, she wished the sidewalk would open up and consume her. "I can explain."

"No need. You were checking up on me because you felt guilty about standing me up all those years ago. You had to make sure I survived the heartbreak to ease your conscience. I'll have you know—I was devastated when you didn't show up for our date."

Wait. What? "Me? Cause you heartache?" Layla laughed. She couldn't help it. Like that would ever happen. Even back then, Shane could have his pick of far more beautiful girls than her. The same held true today. "And you never asked me out. You must be thinking of one of the other girls who swooned at your feet."

"I most definitely did. About a week after we first

met. I remember because I was nervous as hell. I'd never asked a girl out before."

"You didn't ask me out, Shane."

"Yes, I did. I asked you to go fishing with me. You said yes and then you didn't show."

Layla stopped short in the middle of the sidewalk. She gawked at him when he turned to face her. "That was a date?" She remembered him asking all those years ago, but never put two and two together.

"Of course. What did you think it was?"

Anything but a date. Boys never wanted to go out with the gangly metal-mouth Williams. They all drooled over beautiful Zara who never suffered through "the awkward stages" in her life. "You said a bunch of you were going fishing and asked if I wanted to come. That was *not* a date."

"I beg to differ." He arched a brow and cast a challenging glance down his patrician nose.

"You have dinner on a date. Go to the movies even, or a party. Not to the local watering hole."

"Okay, so I was a little dorky back then. In my defense, I was only fourteen." He cracked a thousand-megawatt smile that almost made her go weak in the knees. "And you did say you'd go with me." His expression turned curious. "How come you didn't show?"

She'd wanted to go. More than anything in the world. "I...didn't know how to fish. Still don't know how." She hadn't wanted to make a fool of herself. So she'd ditched him. *Idiot, idiot, idiot.* "I'm sorry."

Shane's low, sexy chuckle sent her heart fluttering. "Don't worry about it." He waved off her concern. "It was years ago. Besides—" His wolfish grin appeared again. He clamped his hands over his chest. "My broken heart has healed."

Broken heart, my ass. Layla mock punched him in the arm. "Right," she scoffed. She started walking again. "Come on. We've got donations to pick up."

They continued on their way, stopping a few minutes later in front of the boutique.

"It was a date," he whispered in her ear when she yanked open the door.

He'd wanted her. Not any of the other popular gorgeous girls. A rush of warmth flooded through her.

"It was," he insisted.

Layla chuckled. "You'll have to do better than that next time."

His slow sexy smile sent her pulse racing. "Oh, I will."

Oh, boy. She was in big trouble now.

"You okay, Wall Street?" The sun sank low in the late afternoon sky as Duncan drove the ambulance back to the medical services building.

No. How could he be when a kid's life hung in the balance? Shane rubbed a hand at the back of his neck. What could have possessed the kid to drive eighty miles per hour on the back roads in the winter? Talk about stupid.

Okay, yeah. He'd done some foolish things in his teens, too. Most kids did. It was part of growing up. He'd been lucky enough to survive, and this kid… God, they'd needed a winch to pry the car away from the tree.

"I know what you're going through. The first time you go out on a call like that…" Duncan's voice trailed off and he stayed quiet for a moment, then he added, "You can't question yourself. The what-ifs will eat you alive if you let them."

Yeah. That about summed it up.

Duncan pulled the ambulance into the bay and killed the ignition. He turned to Shane and locked his gaze on him. "The harsh reality is, we can't save everyone."

His logical mind understood this, but…

"You did everything you could."

The ER doctor had told him the same thing, but that didn't stop the self-doubt from creeping in.

"You know what I could use right about now?" Duncan asked. "A beer and a game of pool. You in?"

"Aren't you and Mark supposed to meet with Layla now?"

Duncan's brows furrowed. "How did you know?"

"We were collecting donations for the silent auction when you texted her and she mentioned it." He couldn't help thinking about how much he'd enjoyed spending those few hours together.

"It wasn't a date." Her words floated through his mind. Shane smiled to himself. She had a point.

"You'll have to do better next time." Could she want a next time? Did he want a next time?

"Mark can handle it. He'll understand." Duncan's voice tore him from his thoughts.

Shane blinked. His current reality crashed down on him.

"No need." He appreciated Duncan's attempt to divert his attention. "I've got a date with a crowbar." Kitchen demolition would distract him, and the physical activity would make him tired enough to drop off the minute his head hit the pillow. He'd need that tonight.

"Okay. Let's restock this baby so we can both get outta here."

Shane nodded. The sooner the better.

Shane stared at the kitchen. He'd pretty much gutted the place and in record time. Four and a half hours was a new personal best for him considering he'd completed the demolition alone. It was time to call it a night— after he finished cleaning up.

He hauled the last of the cabinets out to his detached garage. He'd salvage what he could for storage and take the rest to the dump later in the week.

Shane walked the short distance back to the house, stopping when a car pulled in the driveway. A woman hopped out a moment later. "Layla." The full moon provided more than enough light for him to recognize her.

"Hi." She came toward him.

"Hey. What are you doing here?" His voice came out more accusing than curious. Damn. Shane dragged a hand through his hair and let out a frustrated sigh. "Sorry, I didn't mean to bark at you." That was the last thing he'd wanted to do.

Layla stopped a couple of feet away from where he stood. "I'm not planning on staying. Just wanted to drop this off." She handed him the thermal take-out bag clenched in her left hand.

His brows drew together in a deep V. "What's this?"

A hint of a smile graced her face. "It's one of those burgers you like."

She brought him a burger. "Why?"

"Heard about the accident you got called out on. I figured…" Layla lifted one petite shoulder and waved her hand in the air. "Well, food is what I do. I just wanted you to have something…comforting. Anyway… I guess I should leave you to it. Good night." She turned and headed back to her car.

He unzipped the bag and peeked inside. The heady aroma of spiced beef filled his nostrils. His mouth watered. Stomach growled. He couldn't remember when he'd last eaten. How had she known what he'd needed? Shane noticed another container and lifted the lid. Several chocolate-chip cookies and a pile of Hershey's Nuggets sat inside.

He hadn't been serious when he'd asked her to make him chocolate-chip cookies, but she'd made them for him anyway, and she remembered he liked all things Hershey. "Hold on." Shane jogged to her car. "Do you have time to come in? I can make coffee." He couldn't send her away when she'd been this thoughtful.

"I don't want to intrude."

He shook his head. "You're not intruding. I could use a break." If he were honest with himself, he wanted her company.

Her smile warmed him and set his heart beating at a rapid pace. "I'd love a cup." Layla exited her Mini Cooper and followed him inside.

"Let me take your coat," he said when they stepped

into the front entry. He set the thermal bag on the floor and extended his hand. A spark of electricity jolted through him when their fingers touched. Shane sucked in a deep breath and released it slowly. He hung her coat in the hall closet. Grabbing another hanger, he hung his parka next to hers. "Come on." Shane motioned for her to follow him. "I want to show you the living room." He couldn't wait to see her reaction to what he'd done since they'd painted last Sunday.

"Did you do more—" Layla stopped speaking when he flicked the switch and light flooded the room. "Oh, wow." She walked in and rested her hand on the back of the new sofa he'd purchased. She turned back to him, a stunned expression on her face.

"What do you think?" he asked when she said nothing more. His insides jumped and jittered as he waited for her response.

"I don't know where to look first. This is perfect." Layla ran her hand along the back of the plush dark gray sectional sofa he'd placed in the center of the room in front of the fireplace. "And this," she gestured to the taupe-and-gray-print area carpet in front of the sofa. "Much, much better than the ratty old rug that was here before."

"I'll say," he agreed.

"And the wood floor… Oh, Shane. It's stunning. You did a phenomenal job refinishing the boards."

He grinned. "Thanks."

"The whole room looks awesome. I love it."

Her admiration filled him with satisfaction.

"Have you done anything else?" She walked toward

the back of the room where it connected to the dining room.

"Actually—" He followed behind, bumping into her when she stopped short.

"Ho-ly cow!" She stared at the empty space that used to hold his kitchen. "When did you do this?"

"Today." His insides twisted. He'd almost forgotten the day he'd had. Almost.

"I understand." Layla gave a sage nod. "As distractions go, I'm sure all of this—" she gestured around the empty space "—took your mind off—" She gave an awkward wave of her hand.

In a move that surprised him, Layla grasped his hand and gave it a gentle squeeze. "I can't claim to know what you're going through right now." She lifted her gaze to meet his. "But I wanted you to know that I'm here… If you need anything."

He'd been wrong regarding her. She wasn't an uptight, self-centered New York socialite who couldn't give a rat's ass about anyone but themselves. Far from it. Just look what she'd done for him tonight. Her care and compassion warmed his heart.

"Thanks. That means a lot."

"Anytime." She released his hand.

Her smile sent a rush of warmth through him. He sucked in a breath, to steady his racing heart. "How about I get you that coffee I promised."

Layla peered around the empty room. "Where are you going to make it?"

Shane tapped the side of his head and smiled. "I thought of that." He motioned for her to follow him.

He walked around the corner and into the hall. "The new pantry." He pointed to the converted closet. Opening the door, he reached inside and grabbed the bag of coffee and two mugs. "I moved the coffeepot to the dining room table."

"I hope you moved the microwave there, too. You'll starve otherwise." Her soft chuckle sent a zing of excitement through him.

"Speaking of which." Shane walked through the kitchen and into the entryway. He leaned down and grasped the container Layla had given him earlier with his free hand. "I'm hungry." He strode to the table. After setting everything on it, Shane grabbed the pot and prepared the coffee. "What about you? Would you join me?"

"No, thanks. I ate at the restaurant before I came here. The coffee is fine." Layla sat in an empty chair at the table. "Please, eat before it gets any colder."

Shane sat adjacent to her and removed the contents from the bag. "This looks delicious." He bit into the burger and let out a groan. "So good."

"Glad you like it."

"So, how did things go today?" He should have asked her earlier. No. He should have called her when he got off shift. Instead, he'd wallowed in misery, pitying himself. "I'm so sorry I couldn't get there. I promised—"

"I understand. It's not like you blew me off, or anything like that." She shot him a sassy grin.

He laughed. He couldn't help it. She was making fun of herself for doing the same thing to him all those years ago.

"I'm happy to report the restaurant was packed. I haven't gone through all the receipts yet, but I'd bet we generated the extra two thousand you indicated we needed."

Shane lifted his hand and gave her a high five. "Way to go."

"I'm going to do this, Shane." She grasped his hand and squeezed it. "I'm going to save my restaurant. That bastard won't win."

He caught the moisture in her eyes before she lowered her head. "Bastard?" Shane lifted her chin and waited until her gaze settled on him. "Want to tell me about it?"

"Do you really want to know?"

"Yes. Being there for someone should go both ways." He pointed to her and back at himself.

"Okay." Layla straightened her shoulders.

"I met Antoine three years ago at a dinner party held by mutual friends. He was tall and James Bond handsome."

Shane arched a brow. "That good, huh?"

"Yeah," she said matter-of-factly. "We hit it off right away. Of course, we had a lot in common, both of us being professional chefs. The more I got to know him, the better I liked him. I thought we had this connection, you know? We seemed to be on the same page about what was important in life.

"Was it like that for you with your ex?" she asked.

Shane stiffened.

"Sorry—I shouldn't have pried."

He relaxed. "You're not prying." He wanted her to

know. "I'd say it was more like instant attraction for Melinda and me."

"There is something to be said about that." She laid her arms on the table. His pulse kicked up a notch when her hand accidently brushed against his.

Shane chuckled. "Yes, there is."

"Anyway, it wasn't long before things turned serious between Antoine and me." Layla sighed. "We moved in together a couple of months after we started dating. In my defense, I thought I was in love with him."

Shane shook his head. "I'm not judging you." How could he? "I asked Melinda to marry me six months after we met. We tied the knot a short time later."

She shot an enquiring glance at him. "If you got married that fast, there must have been something more than sex between you. Unless…"

"No. She wasn't pregnant. We were both young and wanted to wait a few years." Good thing too, considering how short they stayed together. "As for the bond you talked about, you're right. At least I believed we were in sync with what each other wanted. I learned quickly that 'we' meant Melinda."

"You sacrificed your dreams to make her happy."

"Yes." They'd lived in a posh condo in Manhattan— the polar opposite of the smalltown community life he preferred. Entertained her friends not the "Neanderthals" he like to watch sports with.

As for his career…being a paramedic's wife wasn't part of Melinda's agenda. She liked high society living, something he couldn't give her on a paramedic's salary. "But you can only do that for so long." It had taken him two years to come to that conclusion.

Layla nodded. "A relationship won't work if one person does all the taking and never gives."

She seemed to understand. "Is that what happened with you and Antoine?"

A thoughtful expression crossed her face. "If you'd asked me that when Antoine and I split eleven months ago, I would have said no, but looking back…yes. At least in part."

"What do you mean?" he asked.

"I've *always* wanted to own my own restaurant. Since I was a little kid."

He nodded. She'd told him as much.

"Antoine wanted the same. I thought we shared the same dream."

"But you didn't?"

"I think it was more that we had different visions of that dream."

"How so?"

"About a month after we moved in together, an opportunity came up to purchase a place. It was exactly what I had wanted. A cozy little bistro right in the heart of Paris, but it was more than we could afford." She shook her head. "I was so disappointed, but a couple of days later, Antoine came home and told me he'd borrowed the money from his parents and bought it.

"Things were wonderful in the beginning. I did most of the cooking. My dishes earned us three Michelin stars. Chez Antoine got rave reviews. All was right with the world."

Shane arched a brow. "He named the place after himself?"

Layla gave a derisive laugh. "I know, but I was just so happy that we were opening the bistro that I didn't object when he proposed the name to me."

"When did things change?" Obviously, they must have or she wouldn't be here.

"I can't give you one concrete thing that happened. It was a lot of little things over time, like… He'd claim all the credit for the restaurant's success, and sometimes he'd refer to the place as his, which technically was true, but it bothered me."

"I can see why. You were supposed to be partners."

"Yeah, except I started to feel more like an employee."

"He took advantage of you. Is that when you decided to buy your grandfather's place? Because you realized you couldn't keep making sacrifices."

A shudder ran through her. "No. That happened after."

"After what?" he asked.

She shot him a derisive glance. "After I learned how wrong I was about us being on the same page." Layla sucked in a breath and blew it out slowly. "Did I mentioned Antoine and I got engaged?"

Shane shook his head. "No. You left that little detail out."

She let out a soft chuckle. "We did. About a year after we opened the restaurant. I was happy—mostly." She shook her head. "When the little stuff started to bother me, I thought, things can't be perfect all of the time. Antoine loves me and I love him. We'd work it out.

"Anyway, fast forward a year to right before 'the big day.' I had checked into the hotel where my family was staying so I could spend time with them while they were in Paris." She paused and licked her lips. "The day before the wedding, I realized I'd forgotten the pearl necklace I wanted to wear with my wedding dress at my apartment. Mom and Nonny hadn't seen our new place so we went over. Antoine must not have heard us come in."

Ah, hell. He knew what was coming next, and he wanted to cringe.

"*We*—Mom, Nonny, Zara and me—found him in bed with another woman."

Shane sucked in a breath. It would have been bad enough to discover Antoine's infidelity, but having others witness his adultery… "I'm sorry that happened to you." Shane laced his fingers with hers.

She looked at him with a dumbfounded expression on her face. "He fired me when I called off our wedding. I guess he saw me as just an employee, after all."

Bastard was too good a word to describe the ass wipe, Shane thought.

"Needless to say, I jumped at the chance to buy my grandfather's place when he offered it to me." Layla shook her head. "I thought, I'll show Antoine. La Cabane de La Mer would be bigger and better than his place would ever be."

She stayed quiet for a moment, then added, "Not the best motivation for a successful business venture."

"No," he agreed, but he understood better her motivations and why she'd ended up in such a mess.

"You must think I'm a complete idiot. I certainly feel like one."

"No. Absolutely not. I think you're brave. You've picked up the pieces and built a whole new life for yourself. You pursued your dream. Okay, there've been a few hiccups along the way, but you're determined to fix things. You're a smart woman, Layla." Shane brushed a lock of hair away from her face. Their gazes connected. His breath hitched. "Beautiful."

A slow smile crossed her face. Layla leaned toward him. The heady scent of honey and lavender flooded his senses. He closed his eyes and breathed in the intoxicating fragrance. A slow languid warmth filled his chest.

Her warm soft lips brushed against the rough scruff of his cheek. The featherlight touch sent a flurry of sparks over the surface of his skin. Anticipation hummed and buzzed inside him.

He opened his eyes. Layla's gaze locked on him. A faint pink blush covered her neck and rose up to highlight her cheeks.

"I, ah…" Layla worried her bottom lip. "Should get going."

He found the hint of shyness quite endearing. Oh, who was he kidding? He found everything about her appealing. "You haven't had your coffee yet."

"Can I get a rain check?"

"Oh, yes. Most definitely." Shane stood and tossed her a wicked grin. "Let me get your coat for you." He walked into the front entry and grabbed her coat from the closet, holding it for her to slip into. Shane grabbed his parka and opened the front door. He gestured for her to precede him. "I'll walk you to your car."

"You don't have to do that."

"Oh, yes I do." Shane wanted that *next time* with her.

They walked the short distance to her Mini Cooper in silence.

Layla opened the door with her key fob, and turned to face him.

"Are you busy Friday night?" he asked. He hoped her sous-chef was still covering the dinner service.

Surprise flickered in her gaze. "No. Why?"

He grasped her hands in his and waited until her gaze settled on him. "Will you have dinner with me?"

A slow smile spread across her pretty face. "I'd love to."

His heart raced faster than a train traveling at top speed. "Great. I'll pick you up at seven." Shane leaned in and touched his lips to hers. Oh, yes. *Next time* couldn't come fast enough.

Layla groaned as his mouth covered hers. He tasted better than the finest chocolate. Better than any gourmet meal or fine wine she'd ever tasted. His lush lips nibbled, stroked with a tantalizing persuasion she couldn't resist. Everything inside her turned soft. She sighed and slipped her arms around his neck, giving herself up to the exquisite pleasure of his kiss.

He eased away long moments later.

Layla stared up at him. She was pretty sure a goofy grin spread across her face. "Good night, Shane."

"Good night. And thanks for coming over tonight." He brushed his lips over hers once again. "Drive safe."

He opened her car door and she slipped behind the steering wheel.

"One more thing," he said as she was about to close her door.

"What's that?"

"Friday is a date." He flashed a wolfish grin. "I wanted to be clear on the matter."

She let out a soft chuckle and started the car. "Good to know."

Shane closed the door and waved.

Her heart pounded wildly in her chest. Suddenly, she couldn't wait for Friday to arrive.

Chapter Eight

Layla paced back and forth in the kitchen. She glanced at her watch. One in the afternoon and only a couple of dozen customers thus far today. Instead of increasing the number of patrons since they'd started serving lunch two days ago, the quantities had declined. She'd barely broken even yesterday. Today, if things didn't improve fast... *Don't go there.* She couldn't.

"Table seven asked for you." Emily walked into the kitchen and moved to the cooler. Grabbing two salads, she placed them on her tray.

Layla straightened her toque and her whites. "I'll go and say hi now. Which orders were theirs?" She always made sure to know what meals her customers ordered. It made for a more personal connection when she spoke with them. It wouldn't be hard for Emily to remember. She'd only waited on six customers in the last thirty minutes.

"Haven't ordered yet. They wanted to talk to you first."

"Okay, thanks." She gestured for Emily to precede her out of the kitchen. Layla smiled as she approached the group of four sitting at table seven. "Hi, Mark. Everyone. It's good to see you all."

"Hi, Layla. You said drop by anytime so here I am." The EMS director gestured to the others at the table. "Thought I'd bring a few members of the team along. You know Duncan." Mark gestured to the tall, stocky man to his right. "This is Ursula Smith." He pointed to the woman who sat to his left. "And Terry Conway." He pointed to the other woman at the table.

"It's nice to meet both of you." Layla gave a wide grin. "Welcome everyone. I'm happy you're here. What can I get for you today?"

"It all looks so good. What do you recommend?" Mark asked.

"Today's special is the croque monsieur." Layla pointed to the sandwich on the menu.

"A ham and cheese on wheat bread." Mark nodded. "I'll take it."

Layla cringed a little at that basic interpretation. Her croque monsieur was much more than a simple ham and cheese sandwich. She always piled thin slices of moist French ham between two slices of fresh homemade bread, toasted to perfection, and the velvety béchamel and Gruyère cheese oozed out all over the place, but she wouldn't argue with him.

"I'll have the same," Ursula said.

"I'll have the coq au vin," Terry added.

"How about you, Duncan?" she asked.

Duncan lifted his blond curly head from the menu and stared at her, a confused expression on his face. "I want the burger Wall Street told me about, but I can't find it on the menu."

"Who are you talking about?" Ursula asked.

Mark chuckled. "Shane Kavanaugh."

"Yeah." Duncan nodded. "He couldn't stop raving about all that juicy meat stuffed with loads of cheese on a fancy bun."

The burger she'd made for him the evening he'd reviewed the restaurant's financials and the other night when she'd stopped by—*the night he kissed me*. And yes, it had been better than she'd ever dreamed. He'd praised her cooking to his colleague? A warm pressure filled her chest.

"That sounds pretty good," Mark agreed. "Can I order that, too?"

"Me, three?" Ursula asked.

"Why can't I find it on here?" Duncan's brows drew together as he studied the menu.

She'd never added it to the menu. It had seemed... sacrilegious to serve a basic burger in an exclusive French restaurant. She peered around the mostly empty dining room. *Give the people what they want*. At least for today. "Don't worry about that." Layla waved off Duncan's concern. She wasn't about to explain. "I'm happy to make them." She had the ingredients required on hand since she'd planned to make chou farci, her favorite rustic stuffed cabbage dish, as an experiment for the dinner menu. But she wouldn't need the cabbage for her burgers.

She motioned for Emily to join her. When Emily arrived at her side, Layla introduced the server who would take their beverage orders while she took care of their meals.

Returning to the kitchen, Layla strode to the refrigerator. She grabbed the ground beef and her secret ingredient sausage, and set the containers on the counter.

Working as fast as she could, she prepared all of the meals. Adding hand-cut fries and a garnish to each of the burger plates, she set the dishes on a tray.

Emily strode into the kitchen to place a new lunch order and eyed the contents of the tray. "New menu item?"

Layla lifted the tray and headed toward the door. "Not a chance." She walked down the hall and back into the dining room, setting the tray on a nearby stand. "Here we go." Layla set the plates on the table.

Mark's eyes widened. "This looks amazing."

"Kavanaugh was right," Duncan said around a mouthful. "Best burger ever."

Ursula held the burger to her mouth and bit in. Her eyes closed and the look on her face... Pure ecstasy.

"This is delicious, too." Fork in hand, Terry gestured to her coq au vin. "You've got to try it." She slid the plate toward Ursula.

Ursula lifted a forkful to her mouth. "Oh, my gosh. Yes. Delicious. I suppose you want to try my burger?" She arched a brow and trained her gaze on Terry.

"Um, yeah." Terry motioned with her hands for Ursula to slide over her plate.

Ursula pulled a face. "Okay, fine, but make it a small bite."

Terry did as Ursula asked. "Yep. It's amazing." She pulled out her cell. "Cal has got to do a segment here. Be right back." She stepped away from the table.

"Who's Cal?" Layla asked.

"Her husband," Mark answered. "He does the What's Cooking segment." At Layla's puzzled expression he added, "On the evening news."

"I've never seen it," Layla confessed. "I mean, I'm usually here for dinner service, so I never get to watch TV at that hour."

"He goes to all the best local restaurants in this part of the state and interviews them," Ursula explained. "The segments run on Tuesdays during the six p.m. news and feature the proprietor's signature dishes."

"You're kidding?" Layla's mouth dropped open. This could be the exposure she'd been looking for.

"Nope." Mark shook his head. "Cal has a huge following and people flock to the places he reviews."

Terry returned to the table, a triumphant smile on her face. "Cal is on board. Expect a call from the news station this afternoon. His assistant will set up a time for him to film the segment and he'll walk you through what to expect."

"Thank you." Layla wanted to jump for joy and scream from the rooftop. Instead, she grasped Terry's hand and shook it. "I really appreciate the endorsement."

"You're welcome. Your food is delicious."

"Please. Sit down and enjoy your meal before it gets cold." Layla gestured to the table. "Signal Emily if you need anything else. Bon appétit."

Head spinning, Layla returned to the kitchen. She couldn't wait to share the good news with Shane tonight.

Layla stared at herself in the bedroom full-length mirror. *No good.* She pulled the navy long-sleeved dress over her head and tossed it. Rummaging through the pile of dresses heaped on her bed, she plucked up the cream-colored two-piece sweater dress and slipped it on.

She stared at the high-waisted, midlength rib knit skirt with the matching long-sleeved crop top. "Bingo." She smoothed the material over her body and shoved her feet into close-toed taupe suede ankle boots. A touch of blush and some lip gloss and... Maybe she should wear her hair up?

The front doorbell dinged.

Layla glanced at her watch. Seven in the evening. Shane was right on time. *Hair down it is.* "Be right there," she called as she hurried toward the entrance.

She opened the door. Shane stood in front of her decked out in a pair of black trousers and a periwinkle dress shirt. *Oh, my.* The breath whooshed out of her.

"Wow. You look fantastic." Shane's gaze swept over her from head to toes.

Her pulse thumped a satisfied beat. "So do you."

"These are for you." He handed her a bouquet of white roses, lilies and mini carnations.

She inhaled their fragrance and smiled. "Oh, they're beautiful. Thank you. Please, come in while I put them in water."

Shane followed her into the living room. "Cute place."

"Thanks. It's small, but it will do for now." She walked into the kitchen. Grabbing a vase from under the sink, she arranged the flowers into a pleasing display and filled it with water. "Where are we going tonight?" she asked. He'd been vague when they spoke yesterday.

A wide grin spread across Shane's face. "Like I said the other night. Dinner. A movie if you're up for it."

It was what he'd already told her. "Care to be more specific?" She arched a brow.

"No." His sexy grin returned. "You'll have to wait and see. Ready to go?"

Anticipation thrummed and zinged inside her. *As ready as I'll ever be.* "Sure. Let's head out." Layla strode to the closet and grabbed her long navy wool coat.

Shane plucked it out of her hands. He held it out for her to slip her arms into the sleeves.

First flowers and now this. His thoughtful gestures warmed her heart. "Thank you."

"You're welcome." His arms circled around her and he pulled her in close.

Her heart beat a rapid tattoo.

Everything inside her turned soft and languid. How could one look, one touch from him set off this deep longing inside her? And this need…

Kiss me. Please. She ached for the sweet press of his lips on hers.

He must have read her mind because he tugged her closer and lowered his head.

Layla melted against him as his lips caressed hers. She welcomed the lazy heat that flowed through her as he nipped and nibbled the hollow at the base of her throat.

Her surroundings faded until it was just the two of them and the sensual dance of their tongues gliding, hands caressing.

Layla wasn't sure how much time passed when he finally—unwillingly if his heavy sigh was anything to go by—eased away from her.

"I've been dying to do that all day." The tips of his ears turned a bright shade of red.

Layla grinned. She couldn't help it. She adored his reluctant admission. What the man could do with his lips. "You know, you don't have to stop on my account." *Feel free to indulge at any time.*

"We won't get out of here if I keep it up, and I promised to feed you. Ready?" Shane crooked his elbow to the side and she slipped her arm through.

She breathed in a steadying breath and smiled. "Yes."

They exited her apartment and headed down the back stairs to Shane's truck.

He opened the door for her, then dashed around and got into the driver's seat.

"Will you do something for me?" Shane asked after he'd slid behind the wheel.

She shot him a curious glance. "What's that?"

"Would you close your eyes until we get where we're going? I want it to be a surprise. I promise it's a short ride. Don't worry," he added when she only stared at him. "I promise I won't take you anywhere bad."

Layla chuckled. "I didn't think you would." The Shane she'd gotten to know this past week wouldn't do anything of the sort. She closed her eyes. "But you've got me really curious. Can you give me a hint? Please?"

"It has a relaxed atmosphere. I think you'll enjoy the food. It's not gourmet, but it's good."

"And it's close by?" *The diner maybe?* It definitely had a relaxed atmosphere.

"That's all I'm saying. You'll find out soon enough." She felt the truck move beneath her as he pulled out of the spot. "Tell me, how was your day?"

"Oh, you're never going to believe this." She told him how her restaurant would be featured on the What's Cooking news segment.

"That's awesome," Shane responded. "I didn't realize Terry's husband worked for the news station. I'm glad they came in today."

"Me, too. This is going to be great exposure for the restaurant."

"Do you know when they're going to shoot the segment?" Shane asked.

"I received a call from the news station this afternoon. They're sending the reporter and a camera crew over tomorrow at noon."

"That soon?"

Layla nodded. "They want to air the segment next Tuesday."

"I'll make sure to be there."

The car stopped.

"Don't open your eyes yet," Shane said. "I want you to keep them closed a little longer. I'll escort you inside."

She heard his door open and shut. Another door opened and the cool evening air blasted over her a moment later.

"Take my hand." Shane grasped hers.

Layla swiveled in her seat, planting both feet on the ground. "Is there any ice?"

"Nope. I made sure to clear it away."

The roar of the ocean sounded and the scent of the sea lingered in the air. She frowned. The diner wasn't close enough to the water to hear the waves crashing on shore. No restaurant was close enough, except hers. "Are we at La Cabane de La Mer?"

Shane's throaty chuckle sent shivers dancing down her spine. "No. Step up."

"Huh?" Layla stopped short. "What do you mean?"

"There are three steps in front of you. We need to climb them. Oh, forget it."

The next thing she knew, Layla felt herself literally swept off her feet and into Shane's arms. "What are you doing?"

"Making sure you don't hurt yourself. Keep your eyes closed."

"Yes, sir." She snaked her arms around his neck and relaxed as he held her safe and secure against his chest.

A grin spread across her face. "I can't wait to see where we are. You've got me stumped."

A blast of heat greeted her a moment later, followed by the savory aroma of seasoned lamb. "It smells fantastic. Where are we? I'm opening my eyes now." She lifted her lashes and peered around. "What are we doing at your place?"

He still held her close and she luxuriated in the feel of her body cradled in the strength of his arms. "You're always cooking for everyone else so I wanted to make you dinner for a change." A tentative smile formed on his face.

"You cooked?" She gazed into his gorgeous blue eyes. "For me?"

She couldn't believe he'd do such a thing, and found herself more touched than she might have expected. He'd really gone out of his way.

For her.

"You can relax and enjoy."

A rush of warmth filled her chest to bursting point. Layla pressed her lips against his cold stubbled cheek and kissed him. "You sweet, sweet man."

Shane grinned. "Welcome to Café Kavanaugh." He lowered her to the ground. "Let me take your coat, mademoiselle."

Layla handed him the garment. "Wait a minute." Her brows furrowed. "How did you cook dinner? Your kitchen was empty when I was here two days ago."

"I bought a new stove and fridge. They delivered them this morning. Cabinets will be here in a few weeks. Now come with me." He grasped her hand and led her into the living room.

A small square table stood in front of the fireplace. White dishes sat atop silver-rimmed charger plates, and silver cutlery flanked each plate. White linen napkins and water and wine goblets completed the setting. Elegant. Intimate. A frisson of pleasure trickled down her spine. "Very nice." She nodded approvingly.

"Milady." Shane pulled out a chair and gestured for her to sit. He produced a lighter and lit the two white tapered candles that sat atop the dark tablecloth. "Shall I light the fire?"

Layla smiled. "Yes, please do."

He moved to the fireplace. Grabbing the remote from the mantel, he pressed a button. Flames burst to life. "Would you like some wine?"

"I'd love some."

"I'll be right back." He disappeared around the corner and returned a few minutes later with a bottle. Shane poured a small portion into her glass. "Is the Pinot Noir to your liking?"

Layla smiled and swirled the dark liquid in her glass. She breathed in the fragrant bouquet. "It smells good." She sipped the wine. Hints of strawberry, tart cherry and cranberry burst into her mouth. "It's delicious."

Shane filled her glass and poured a goblet for himself. Setting the bottle aside, he moved to the seat next to her and sat. "Cheers." He lifted his goblet in the air.

"To an enjoyable evening." Layla clinked her glass against his.

"Are you? Enjoying yourself, I mean?" His gaze locked with hers.

"How could I not? You're spoiling me rotten. You'd better watch out. I could get used to this."

His low chuckle sent a rush of heat through her. Layla swallowed hard. What was happening to her? Okay. That was a silly question. She knew exactly what was happening. She needed to change the subject. Fast. "So, what are we having for dinner?"

"Coming right up." A slow smile formed on his handsome face as he rose from the table and disappeared into the kitchen.

Oh, my. Layla swallowed hard and fanned herself with her hand. It was amazing the way even the sound of his voice was affecting her body. She gulped down the entire glass of water sitting beside her plate, desperate to cool herself. More in control now, she set the glass down and drew in a calming breath.

The sound of a pan hitting the floor echoed from the kitchen. She laughed when Shane uttered a muffled curse.

He appeared a few minutes later. "Here we go." With a flourish, he set a rectangular white serving dish in the center of the table. It held crackers laden with what appeared to be a fig and olive tapenade.

Her eyes widened. "This looks delicious." Layla scooped some of the spread onto a cracker and lifted it to her mouth and bit it. A flood of flavors burst into her mouth. Sweetness, from the fig and the salty brine of the Kalamata olives mixed with a hint of anchovies, capers, olive oil and lemon juice. "It's wonderful." She stuck the remainder of the cracker in her mouth and savored the taste.

"I'm glad you like it."

Layla cocked her head to the side. "Where did you learn to cook like this?"

"I'm self-taught. I figured I'd better learn or I might starve." Shane cleared his throat. "You have a tiny bit of tapenade on your lip."

Heat flooded her face. She touched her napkin to the corner of her mouth. "Did I get it?"

"No. It's on the bottom right."

She rubbed in the area he mentioned.

"Let me." He reached across the table and brushed his thumb over her bottom lip.

Her pulse soared and heat pooled low in her belly.

His gaze met hers. "It's gone."

"Um, thanks." Her insides jumped and jittered.

Shane leaned closer and brushed his lips over hers. "You're welcome."

Frissons of pleasure danced along her spine. Layla scooted closer.

He pressed soft kisses against her forehead, her eyelids and the tip of her nose.

Tiny shivers flickered over her heated skin. How could such fleeting touches create this deep sense of… Desire, yes. She couldn't deny that, but this was more.

"You have the softest skin. I can't stop touching you." He nuzzled a spot at the base of her throat.

"Then don't stop."

"Oh, I won't." He lifted her into his strong sure arms

and carried her to the sofa. Sitting, he placed her on his lap. "This is much better."

She loved the feel of his hard body pressed against her. *Oh, my, yes. Definitely, infinitely much, much better.*

His hands swept over her shoulders and stroked over her back with the lightest of touches, while his lips dotted gentle kisses on her collarbone, her neck and the sensitive spot behind her earlobe.

"You are really good at this touching." Her body tingled from head to toes and she felt as she were floating on air.

His throaty chuckle sent a wave of hot heat rushing through her. "How about the kissing?"

His gaze locked on hers. The breath rushed out of her. No man had ever looked at her with such…adoration. Hunger. Certainly not her ex-fiancé. Lord, why had she never noticed that?

You didn't know what you were missing, that's why. Now you do.

"I think I might need a reminder before I can give you an honest answer."

Shane cupped her face with his palms, stroking her cheeks with his thumbs. Who needed chocolate and wine when she had this?

His mouth covered hers. Parting her lips, she raised herself to meet his kiss.

Tongues tangled; hands caressed. She was so hungry for his touch she thought she might die from the sweet pleasure of it.

Layla closed her eyes. "Okay. I can honestly tell you

the kissing is awesome. As a matter of fact, I would like you to continue both the kissing and the touching. Very much. Please."

"I think I can do that." His lips pressed against hers again. Tingles raced down her spine.

The sound of bells ringing filled the room.

Shane cursed. "That's my alarm." He eased away from her and touched his watch. "Dinner's ready." He gave an ironic smile.

I already have what I want right here. "How offended would you be if I suggest we eat later?" Much, much later.

He grinned. "No offense taken. I'll be right back." Shane set her on the cushion. He raced into the kitchen and returned a moment later. "Had to shut off the oven." He sat and tugged her into his arms again. "Now, where was I?" His fingertips skated over her breasts.

Layla trembled, a moan escaping her lips. "Yes, like that. More of that."

He pulled her close and fastened his lips to hers. The tender touch was almost her undoing.

Layla swung her legs around until her feet hit the floor. She stood, grasping his hand in hers. Smiling, she said, "Let's take this upstairs." Layla couldn't wait to show him how much she wanted him.

Chapter Nine

Shane nudged his bedroom door open with his shoulder and carried Layla inside. Light from the full moon bathed the room with a soft glow. He set Layla down in front of him.

Her gaze met his. "So…" Tension radiated off her in waves.

Maybe she was having second thoughts? He hoped not, but he'd stop if that's what she wanted. "We, ah, don't have—"

"I think you have too many clothes on."

Then again, maybe not. "I can fix that." He'd give her an out just to make sure. "If that's what you want."

Heat flared in her gaze. She looked him in the eyes. "Yes. I definitely want that."

"There's no need to be nervous."

"I'm not." She lowered her gaze. "Okay, maybe a little. It's, um, been a while since I..."

"Me, too." If she could be honest, so could he. Not that he'd been a monk since his divorce. He'd been... selective. "There's nothing to worry about."

"I'm clean," she blurted.

He nodded. "So am I. Now that we've got that settled." Shane grinned. He started to unbutton his dress shirt but she stopped him.

"I'll do it." Her words came out in a rush.

"Okay." He dropped his hands to his sides.

She stepped closer and flicked open one button. Her warm breath felt like a soft caress against his skin. Heat pooled low in his belly.

She worked her way down, releasing one button after another until his chest was bared.

Her emerald eyes glittered in the dim light. "I really want to touch you."

The thought of her hands on him had him hot and hard and so damned ready.

"Please do." His breath hitched when she laid her palms on his skin.

Layla let out a satisfied sigh. "Oh, yeah. This is good."

"Really, really good." He closed his eyes and reveled in the sensations swamping him as she dragged her hands over him.

"I quite like this touching." She stroked his back, his ass.

Shane groaned from the sheer pleasure. "Me, too. Sweetheart. Me, too."

As much as he wanted her to keep going, he needed

to get his hands on her. "It's my turn, again." He flashed his best sexy smile. "We need to get rid of this." He tugged the hem of her pullover.

"I was hoping you'd suggest that." She winked and pulled the sweater over her head, and tossed it on the floor.

Shane grinned. He liked this flirtatious side of her. "Mind if I make this disappear, too?" He brushed his hand over her lacy bra. Her soft cry shot a bolt of electricity jolting through him.

"No." Her voice came out in a breathy whisper. "I don't mind at all."

The air whooshed out of her as he slid the straps down her shoulders.

He released the front clasp and the thin material fell away.

His eyes went wide. He couldn't rip his gaze from her. "You. Are. Exquisite. Absolutely beautiful."

Her smile reached her eyes. She pressed her lips to his. Her sweet kiss was almost his undoing.

"Layla, honey." He brushed his lips along the slim column of her neck, over her collar bone, along the slope of her breasts.

"Shane." Her voice was full of need.

"You like that?" He growled. He was going to explore every inch of her and find out what drove her crazy.

"Yes. Very much." Her gaze turned unfocused. Her head fell back.

"How about this?" Lowering his head, he drew one taut nipple into his mouth.

"Oh, god." She shuddered.

"I love how your body responds to my touch." He craved the sound of her needy cries.

Shane swept her into his arms and strode to his bed. He laid her down gently on the plush comforter. Moving quickly, he removed the rest of their clothes, and joined her.

"So..." Layla gave him a heart-stopping smile.

Shane drew her into his arms.

Tongues tangled. Hands explored; touching, teasing. Frenzied kisses, driving faster, higher.

What was it about this woman that could push him to the edge of reason?

"Now, Shane," Layla cried.

He drove into her one last time and they plunged over the cliff together.

Shane woke the next morning to the scent of honey and lavender, and Layla's warm, supple body entwined with his. He could get used to this.

She mumbled something incoherent, tightening her hold on him.

"Layla?"

She didn't answer and the even rise and fall of her chest indicated she was still asleep.

Shane marveled at how her body fit perfectly with his. He reveled in the sensation of her soft, smooth skin pressed against him. Oh, yeah. He could get used to a lot of things with her, including a repeat of last night.

The sex was... He smiled a satisfied grin.

He noticed the subtle shift in her body and breathing as she came awake. "Good morning."

Layla smiled up at him. "Good morning."

Shane dropped a kiss on her soft lips, and another. Wow, she tasted better than one of her expensive French wines. He groaned when she parted her lips, deepening the kiss. He couldn't get enough of her. How was it that he'd become addicted to her after one night together?

Her body tensed. Something was wrong. Shane eased away.

Dark eyes gazed at him in the dimly lit room. "Why'd you stop?"

"I don't want to, believe me." A certain part of his anatomy would prove his point. Shane sat up in bed and leaned his back against the pillows propped behind him. "Why don't you tell me what's wrong first."

"Wrong? There's nothing wrong." She aimed a sexy smile at him. "Except you're over there." Layla pointed to his side of the bed. "When you should be right here." She patted a spot on the mattress beside her.

Relief flooded through him. He'd thought for a moment she regretted last night. No. She hadn't wanted him to stop. Maybe he'd misread the situation? Shane moved closer. He ran a lazy hand from shoulder to hip. "Are you sure everything is okay? You were totally relaxed a minute ago, but your muscles are tense now."

Layla sat up and sighed. "I'm sorry. The stupid What's Cooking shoot keeps running through my mind. Even though it's the *last* thing I want to think about right now."

Shane let out a soft chuckle. "Ah…" He pulled her into the crook of his arm. "Let's talk about what's worrying you."

She gazed at him, a troubled expression on her lovely face. "So much is riding on this. What if—"

"You are a three Michelin star chef, Layla Williams. Your dishes are out of this world. I know." Shane pointed his thumb at himself. "I've taste-tested your creations." He kissed the top of her head. "Trust me when I say, you've got this. Your cooking will knock that reporter's socks off."

"Thanks." She leaned her forehead against Shane's.

"For what?" he asked.

"For calming the crazies inside my head."

He laughed. "My pleasure. We all get those once in a while."

Layla threw back the blankets and slid from the bed.

Shane blinked. "Where are you going?" He reached for her, but she leaned away.

"It's time to rise and shine, mister." She tossed a saucy grin over her shoulder as she strode around to his side of the bed. "We've got a busy day ahead of us." Grasping his hands, she pulled him to his feet. "We need to shower. No time to waste."

Shane chuckled and scooped her into his arms. "Taking a shower together is a great idea, but I doubt we'll save any time."

Layla hummed as she moved around the restaurant kitchen preparing her coq au vin. She glanced at her watch. The What's Cooking reporter would be here in thirty minutes.

"Hello there." Shane came up from behind her. He wrapped his arms around her middle and dropped a kiss on the side of her cheek.

"What are you doing here? I thought you were going to work on your house for a few hours before your shift." He'd indicated as much when he'd dropped her back at her place after their shower earlier. Heat pooled low in her belly just remembering what they'd done to each other under the hot spray... He'd been right. They hadn't saved any time, but getting to the restaurant had never felt so good.

"I worked all morning." He shrugged. "Can't do any more until my kitchen cabinets arrive so I thought I'd see if I can help with anything here."

A flood of warmth rushed through her. "You're sweet. I'm all set for now. Everything is chopped and ready, but I can't do anything else until Cal Conway arrives. His assistant told me he'll want to capture some film of me preparing one of my dishes."

"How about prep for the rest of the menu? You haven't had a lot of time to prepare this morning."

Layla grinned. "That's because someone made me late." She laughed and pointed the wooden spoon she held in her hand at him.

Shane looked around as if he were trying to spot the culprit. "Who me?" His sexy grin made her go weak in the knees.

She burst out laughing. "Yes, you. Who else would I be talking about? Not that I'm complaining in the least." Layla kissed him. "I'm all set for the segment and for lunch, so now we just wait, I guess."

"It smells fantastic in here. I can't wait to taste everything." Shane pressed his lips to the base of her neck, and let out a low growl. "You taste delicious, too."

Delightful shivers ran down her spine. "You need to stop that. I can't concentrate."

He chuckled when she tilted her head to give him better access.

The alarm on her phone sounded. Layla groaned. She straightened. "I have a quick meeting with Zara to go over the invoices before Cal gets here." They'd started meeting twice a week to make sure everything stayed current.

"Okay. I'll leave you to it."

She exited the kitchen and strode to her office. Layla logged in to the reoccurring Zoom meeting.

"Hi." Zara looked away.

Layla sucked in a deep breath and blew it out slowly. "Hi."

Things remained tense between them and she wasn't sure how to fix them. Yes, Zara had screwed up big time, but so had she. "I think we should—"

"Get started. I've got to get back to work."

She was going to suggest they try to talk things out, but Zara didn't seem interested.

Layla shook her head. She could have fired Zara for what she'd done. Another employer would have, but she couldn't, wouldn't. Zara was family. Twenty-nine years of being sisters meant something to her.

"Okay." She gave a quick nod of her head.

"You already know I made the March loan payment. Thanks for depositing your personal money into the account to cover the difference." Zara's tone was flat and matter-of-fact. "Here's the butcher payment."

Zara's image disappeared and the statement appeared on her screen.

Layla checked off the invoice and placed her copy in the Paid pile on her desk. "That's good. Let's review the next one."

They went through the rest of her invoices without much discussion.

Fifteen minutes later, Zara said, "That's it for now. Talk soon."

The call ended.

She stared at the blank screen. "All righty, then." Layla glanced at her watch. Cal would be here any minute. She closed her laptop and returned to the kitchen.

Five minutes later, a voice called out from the front of the restaurant. She pushed all thoughts of Zara aside.

She met Cal and his cameraperson in the front entry. "Hi." She extended her hand to the reporter. "I'm Layla Williams, chef and owner of La Cabane de La Mer. Thanks for coming."

"Cal Conway." He shook her hand. "This is Eddy Porch. He'll be filming the segment."

Eddy lowered his camera and held out his hand. "Nice to meet you."

Layla smiled. "It's nice to meet you, too."

"Where do you want to start, Cal?" Eddy asked.

"Let's get some footage of the empty dining room. We'll get more later when the patrons arrive."

Layla prayed enough people would come. She'd posted about the segment shoot on the New Suffolk Facebook page and on the restaurant's website and hoped curiosity would be enough to draw people in.

"Which way to the dining room?" Cal peered around the space. "I'm told there's a magnificent view of the ocean from there."

Layla grinned. "Yes, there is. Come with me." She motioned for them to follow her.

"Glass on three sides. Cool." Eddy panned the camera around the space.

"This was the conservatory before my grandfather turned the house into a restaurant. It's always been one of my favorite rooms." Layla peered around. She'd always loved coming in here as a child in the early morning, watching as the sun rose high in the sky and filled the room—filled her—with light and warmth.

Eddy walked to the front of the room and pointed his camera at the ocean.

"So, this is your grandfather's restaurant?" Cal asked.

"No. My grandfather opened his restaurant here about twenty years ago. He retired last year and I opened La Cabane de La Mer last summer." She led her guests to the private dining room next to the bar.

"How did you come up with that name for the place?" Cal followed her. He gazed around the former library with its floor-to-ceiling ornate wood bookcases along the interior wall. "Nice."

"As I mentioned before, this was my grandfather's home for a number of years. He always referred to this place as the sea shack. The French translation is La Cabane de La Mer."

Cal nodded. "The sea shack. I like it. What else is there to see?"

After capturing some videotape in the larger private dining room, they headed to the kitchen.

"I want some footage of you preparing one of your dishes as well as the actual cooking," Cal said.

The kitchen was empty when she stepped inside a moment later. Shane must have slipped out and ducked into her office so as not to be in the way.

Eddy raised his camera and panned around the room.

"Just do what you would normally do when you're making a dish for a customer," Cal instructed. "Eddy will capture what he needs and I'll interview you as you work."

Layla sucked in a deep steadying breath and nodded. *You've got this.* Shane's words from the morning echoed in her head. Yes, she could do this. She'd cooked in one of the finest French restaurants in Paris. Layla strode to the stainless-steel fridge. She grabbed a bunch of carrots. After washing them in the sink, she moved to the prep area and began chopping diagonal slices.

"What dish are you preparing?" Cal asked.

"Coq au vin." Layla added the sliced carrots and the mushrooms, which she'd already prepared, to a frying pan with some olive oil.

"That's French, right?" Cal asked.

"Yes. Loosely translated it means braised chicken

in a butter and wine sauce. I'll add these," she gestured to the frying pan in her hand, "to the rest of the ingredients already simmering in the Dutch oven." Layla walked the short distance to the industrial gas stove. She pointed to the massive cast-iron pot already simmering on one of the burners, and placed the frying pan on another.

"Get a shot of the veggies cooking and make sure you get the sound of the oil sizzling," Cal told Eddy.

They both joined her at the stove.

"In the meantime," Cal added. "Let's see what's in the pot."

Layla lifted the lid. The wonderful aroma of garlic and bacon mixed with chicken, red wine and butter filled the air.

"That smells delicious," Eddy muttered. He held the camera above the pot for a close-up shot, and panned over to the frying pan which was now sizzling.

"Would you like to taste some? I'm happy to prepare a dish for each of you." Layla's cell buzzed in her pocket, but she ignored it. Whoever it was could wait until they finished filming.

"No, thanks. I'm saving myself for one of your other dishes." Cal grinned and waved off her offer. He walked back to the prep area and she and Eddy followed. "What else do you want us to feature?"

Layla hurried back to the stove and ladled boeuf bourguignon into a white soup bowl and added a sprig of fresh parsley on top. She strode to the small table she'd set up in the back of the kitchen complete with a formal place setting. Layla placed the bowl on the white tablecloth to the right of a glass of red wine.

Cal walked over. "Beef stew?" he asked.

Layla nodded, although inside she felt as if he'd stabbed her through the heart. Still, she smiled, knowing that good PR would be priceless. "It's similar." Although her boeuf bourguignon was simmered in both beef stock and a Burgundy wine.

Come on, she told herself. *Who cared what he called it if his story got paying customers into the restaurant?*

Cal stabbed the fork she'd laid out into a piece of beef, carrot and potato. He lifted it to his mouth. Looking at the camera, he smiled and said, "Delicious."

Layla presented her croque monsieur next.

"Anything else you want me to film?" Eddy asked.

"Yeah." Cal turned his attention to Layla. "Let's get some footage of that burger you're so famous for."

"Burger?" Her brows drew into a deep V.

"Yes. The one my wife's friend Ursula raved about. I'm sure the viewers will want to see that, and I can't wait to taste it."

Layla stared at him, dumfounded. He wanted to feature a burger? "Okay." She wouldn't argue with him. "Coming right up." Turning, she strode to the fridge. Her phone buzzed again and she let it go to voice mail. She stopped midstride when one of her waitstaff rushed into the kitchen.

"We've got a—" Sam began.

Shane appeared a moment later. "A nearly full restaurant. We need you out there." He shot Sam a knowing look and gestured toward the door.

"But…" Sam's mouth gaped.

"Is everything okay?" Cal's gaze shot from Sam to Shane to Layla.

"Perfect. We just wanted to give you a heads-up that orders will start coming in soon," Shane answered. He shot another look at Sam and turned to leave.

Sam followed him out.

Layla wasn't sure what that was all about, but she couldn't worry about it now. Her waitstaff could handle the dining room. Right now, she needed to make the best burger ever. "I'll need a few minutes to prep," she told Cal.

"Let's get some shots of the customers while we wait," Eddy suggested.

Cal nodded and he and Eddy exited the kitchen.

Layla prepared the patty and fries. Meal in hand, Layla exited the kitchen in search of Cal. She froze when she stepped into the dining room. Shane wasn't kidding. Every table was filled, and several people were waiting in the entrance area to be seated. It appeared her Facebook and website posts had worked.

She spotted Sam at one of the tables, but where was Jack? Her other server should have arrived twenty minutes ago, when the restaurant had opened. She pulled her cell from her pocket and noticed the missed calls from Jack. It didn't take a genius to figure out Jack wasn't coming in. That must have been why Sam had rushed into the kitchen earlier with that look of panic in her eyes. Her stomach roiled. There was no way one person could handle this volume of people.

Shane came toward her dressed in one of her spare

waitstaff outfits. He flashed one of his devastating smiles. "Jack's car wouldn't start. It's fixed now and he's on his way. Don't worry. I've got you covered until he arrives."

"Thanks." He really was a great guy. "How about dinner tonight?" She'd make him something extra special to repay his kindness.

"How about tomorrow instead? I have to work late tonight."

"No worries. Tomorrow it is."

Shane waggled his brows. "Got any good recipes for leftover lamb?"

The dinner he'd prepared for her last night, but had never gotten around to eating because they'd been too busy pursuing other delights. A delectable shiver danced along her spine. Layla gave him her best sexy grin. "I think I can come up with something."

"It's a date. Gotta go and take orders before the customers revolt." He hurried off.

"Oh, man. That looks great." Eddy lifted his camera and aimed it at the plate in her hand.

"Yes, it does." Cal sat at the one empty table and gestured for Layla to set the meal atop the surface. "But the proof is in the pudding." He picked up the burger with both hands.

Eddy refocused his camera on Cal.

Cal bit into the burger and groaned. "Fantastic." He locked his gaze on the camera. "This is out of this world. You've got to try this for yourselves. I guarantee you won't be disappointed." After a beat, he added, "I think we've got everything we need."

Layla nodded. "Okay. Thanks again for coming."

"You're welcome." Cal dunked a fry into the dipping sauce she'd provided. Lifting the fork to his mouth, he bit off a chunk. "My wife was right. You've got great food here."

Relief flooded through her. "Thank you. I'm glad you've enjoyed what you tasted."

Cal rose from the table. "Can I get this to go?" He gestured to the remaining burger and fries. "It's really delicious."

Layla smiled a mile-wide grin. "Absolutely."

"Actually, can I get five more? I'd love my colleagues at the station to sample these as well."

She'd be foolish to say no. "Sure. I'll have them ready in ten minutes."

Cal nodded. "Great. I'll wait out front for them. Oh, and the segment will air on Tuesday."

"Wonderful." Her smile broadened. "I can't wait to see it."

Shane poked his head into Layla's office. "I've got to go now. There are only a few tables finishing up. Jack's here and you should be all set."

She stood and came out from behind her desk. "Thanks for your help today. I don't know what we would have done without you." Layla wrapped her arms around his neck and kissed him.

"You're welcome." He leaned his forehead against hers.

"This is nice." Layla sighed.

"Yes." One more minute before he had to leave. He

closed his eyes and savored this…connection he felt when he held her in his arms.

Someone knocked on her door.

He released her. "I should go."

"Will I see you tomorrow?"

"You'd better believe it." He pulled her into his arms again for one last satisfying kiss, and turned to leave.

Shane exited out the back door and hopped into his truck. He hummed along with the radio as he drove the short distance from the restaurant to the EMS building.

The alarm blared as he entered the structure, signaling an incoming call. He headed straight to the garage bay and the ambulance.

"353 Pine Avenue, New Suffolk," Duncan said as he hopped into the driver's seat.

Shane froze. "That's La Cabane de La Mer."

"Hell," Duncan grunted. He shoved the key in the ignition and started the ambulance.

Was Layla okay? His heart raced as they drove the short distance to her place.

Shane jumped from the passenger side the moment they arrived and raced to the back of the ambulance. He and Duncan rolled out the gurney. Tossing the equipment on top, they hurried to the main entrance.

The door opened and Layla appeared.

She wasn't hurt. *Thank God.*

"One of our customers is complaining of chest pains." She motioned for Shane and Duncan to follow her.

They pushed the gurney into the dining area. Only two customers remained. Shane's jaw nearly hit the ground when the younger of the two men turned his attention to him. What was Jax Rawlins doing here? He couldn't remember the last time he'd seen him in New Suffolk. Shane glanced at the man slumped in the seat next to Jax. Gary Rawlins. Jax rarely visited his father. What was going on?

Jax rushed toward him. "Shane. My father was complaining about his heart."

He nodded and approached the table. "Hi, Gary. Do you remember me?" Shane took his vitals.

The older man looked up, his pallor faded somewhat, nearly gray. His voice was a bit weak and he was clearly in pain. "Yeah, you're Shane."

"That's right. I'm an EMT. I want you to relax. I'm here to help. Can you tell me what's wrong with you?"

"We were in the middle of eating our meals when he started feeling sick to his stomach. Told me his back and jaw ached," Jax said.

"I called 9-1-1 when he told me," Sam added.

Classic heart attack symptoms. "How are you feeling now?" Shane directed his question to Gary.

"Chest pain. Real bad." Sweat covered Gary's ashen face.

Shane noted the shortness of breath. "I'm going to give you some oxygen." He placed the mask over Gary's face.

"Let's get him on the gurney, and I'll set up for an ECG." Duncan moved the equipment to the empty table.

An echocardiogram would confirm if the symptoms Gary was experiencing were due to a heart attack. He and Duncan transferred the patient to the gurney.

"This will help with the pain." Shane administered a morphine IV.

"ECG is done." Duncan returned the equipment to the container.

"Is he having a heart attack?" Jax asked.

"The ER doctor will have to confirm it, but yes, that appears to be the case." Duncan turned his attention to Shane. "Let's get him to the hospital."

"I'll meet you there." The anxious expression on Jax's face tore at his heart.

"Okay." His questions about what Jax and Gary were doing at Layla's restaurant would have to wait.

Shane guided the gurney through the empty restaurant toward the exit. He caught a glimpse of Layla. He sent up another prayer of thanks that she was okay. If she'd been hurt…

He shuttered. This thing with her… It was supposed to be… Fun. Easy.

He didn't do serious. Couldn't. Serious held consequences he couldn't handle.

Chapter Ten

Make it stop. Eyes still closed; Shane groped for his alarm clock. All he wanted was a few more hours of shut-eye after the long shift he'd had last night. After he and Duncan had taken Gary Rawlins to the hospital and returned to the station, all had been quiet—until eleven thirty, anyway. Wasn't it just his luck a call came in right before his shift ended? It was after two in the morning by the time he'd flopped into bed.

He slammed a hand on the clock, hard, but the incessant buzzing wouldn't stop.

Shane opened his eyes and breathed out a resigned sigh. A beam of sunlight streamed into his bedroom through a crack in the blackout curtains.

The buzzing continued, and he realized the sound emanated from his phone. He was going to kill whoever kept calling or texting him. Shane snatched it off the bedside table and glanced at the screen. Okay, he'd forgive Layla for waking him at…eight in the morning. A smile crossed his face. It wasn't that early.

He unlocked the phone and opened the message. An image of a large platter stacked with what he assumed were crepes covered with powdery sugar filled his screen. Small bowls filled with peanut butter, what looked like chocolate frosting and a red sauce that could be made from strawberries sat on the edge of the platter. He scrolled down and found another image. This one, of a tray of croissants. Yet another image showed a giant stack of pancakes with blueberries and raspberries piled on top.

Today's breakfast feast, her message said.

Looks fantastic, Shane texted back. Did you save some for me? He added a smiley face emoji.

You betcha, came her quick reply.

Shane hopped out of bed. Be over in ten.

How about you open your front door instead?

Shane strode to the bedroom window and yanked open the curtains. He peered out. Sure enough, Layla stood on his front lawn. She smiled and waved at him.

He couldn't believe it. It was probably the sweetest thing any woman—hell, maybe anyone—had ever done for him. Shane grinned. "Be right down."

He grabbed a sweatshirt and tugged it on as he hurried down the stairs. Grabbing a pair of sneakers from the front closet, he jammed his feet into them, and opened the door. Layla held six thermal carriers, three in each hand.

"Hi." She beamed a brilliant smile at him.

"Hi." Shane was sure he wore a goofy grin. "Let me help you with those."

"Thanks." She handed him three of the carriers.

A delicious aroma filled the air. Shane drew in a deep breath. "It smells great. Are there more bags in the car?"

"Nope. This is everything." She stepped into the front entry and closed the door.

"Let me take your coat."

Placing her containers on the floor, Layla slid her arms from it and revealed a long navy ribbed knit dress. The clingy material showed off her curves to perfection. Shane drew in a breath. "You look lovely."

Her lips curved into a brilliant smile. "Thank you."

Shane shifted the carriers to his left hand and accepted her coat in his right.

"I'll take these to the table." She lifted the straps of the containers she'd set on the floor.

"Okay. I'll be there in a minute." He lifted the coat in his hand. "Let me hang this up first."

He joined her at the table a moment later. "I'll get some plates."

"No need." Layla opened one of the carriers and removed two white plates with gold rims. "I brought everything we need."

He stood, mesmerized, as she extracted platters heaped with stacks of food and set them on the table. "What's the occasion?"

"I wanted to thank you for your help at the restaurant yesterday during the What's Cooking segment shoot. Your quick thinking saved the day." She gave a shy smile and looked away. "And I wanted to see you again. I, ah…couldn't wait until tonight. Hence breakfast."

Shane stepped closer to her. He lifted her chin and waited until her gaze settled on his. "Yeah?"

She nodded and her cheeks flushed a delicate shade of pink.

Shane pulled her into his arms and pressed his lips to hers.

"Oh." Layla shivered and wrapped her arms around his neck. She deepened the kiss.

Shane's pulse pounded. His breaths came in quick, sharp pants. What was it about this woman, who, up until a few weeks ago, he hadn't seen in years? She'd invaded his thoughts, haunted his dreams—he found himself longing for her kisses. He couldn't get enough of her. "Breakfast will have to wait." The only thing he wanted now was to sink deep inside her and find the sweet release only she could give him.

He scooped her into his arms and let out his own groan when her curves pressed against his. She pulled his head down to hers and her tongue tangled with his.

Shane strode to the stairs.

"Where are you taking Layla?" a voice asked.

He froze, every muscle in his body going rigid. "Kiera. What are you doing here?"

"Hi, Uncle Shane." Brooke rushed through the front

door followed by his oldest niece, Aurora. "Why are you carrying Layla?"

"Guys, I told you—" Mia appeared. She gawked at Shane. "Sorry. I told them to wait for me."

"Yeah, Kiera," Aurora said. "We were supposed to wait for Mom."

"I waited, but then I saw Uncle Shane coming." Kiera pointed to the slim glass panes set on either side of the wood door frame. "I couldn't wait to show him, so I opened the door. Did you trip and hurt your foot like Brooke did last week?" Kiera asked Layla. "Is that why Uncle Shane is carrying you?"

Mia burst out laughing.

Crap. Heat invaded Shane's cheeks.

"Come on, girls." Mia motioned toward the door. "We'll come back later when Uncle Shane isn't busy."

"But Mom, you said we could show Uncle Shane our new fishing poles!" Kiera held her pole out for Shane to see.

"No, it's okay. Please don't leave on my account." Layla wriggled and whispered, "Put me down," in his ear.

He lowered her to the ground, mourning the loss of her warm supple body pressed against him.

"These are awesome." Layla inspected each girl's pole. "I bet you'll catch lots of fish with these."

The attention she gave his nieces warmed his heart. Melinda would never put up with their antics.

"Do you like fishing?" Kiera asked Layla. "You can come with us later today when Mom takes us to the pond."

"Guys, it's still a little too cold out to go fishing," Shane said.

"Nah—hah." Brooke shook her head. "Mom said it's gonna be forty-five degrees today. Mom's gonna take us to the pond so Layla can come with us."

Shane couldn't miss the surprise that flickered across Layla's face.

"Thanks for the invitation, girls." She hugged each of his nieces. "That sounds like fun, but I don't know how to fish."

Kiera waved off her concern. "It's easy."

"Girls—" Mia began.

"It's okay, Mom. We can teach Layla." Kiera pointed at her sisters and to herself.

"I could teach you, too." Shane sent her what he hoped passed for a winsome smile. "That is if I'm invited."

Brooke rolled her eyes. "Of course you are."

"Great." He high-fived his niece. Turning to Layla, he asked, "What do you say?"

Shane caught Layla's glance. Standing before her now, he felt as hopeful as the boy who'd asked her out all those years ago. He realized only now how much he'd hoped she would say yes back then, but also how afraid he'd been she might say no. She could have gone out with any of the rich kids at the country club, or in her family's circle. He knew that, and so when he did ask her out he'd made it vague—on purpose. Maybe to make it easy for her to turn him down?

Maybe he was doing the same thing again now.

After all, inviting her out with his family for a day was more like a challenge than a date, wasn't it?

She'd told him she couldn't believe he'd want her when he could choose any of the prettier and more popular girls who swooned over him. But she didn't know the truth—that those girls, and later, those women, had never really seen who he was. Not the way she had.

Shane remembered Layla telling him she'd been afraid to take a chance on him all those years ago, but he could see in the openness of her gaze that she wasn't afraid anymore. "Well?"

She smiled. "I say yes. And Shane—just so we're clear, it's a date."

Layla's joyous smile melted his heart.

Layla peered out the window as Shane pulled his truck into one of the many open spaces in the parking lot. "So, this is Long Pond." She stared at the leafless trees and the old wooden picnic tables that sat in the now brown grass.

"You've never been here before?" Shane pocketed the key fob and turned his attention to her.

"No. Not that I can remember." She shot Shane a curious glance. "Where's the water?"

"It's about a five-minute walk from here." Shane pointed to a path that sliced through a grove of trees. "Come on. I'll show you." He hopped out and grabbed the gear from the backseat.

They walked across the parking lot and stepped through the opening. The ground crunched beneath her feet as they made their way. The smell of dirt and old leaves tickled her nose and cool crisp air surrounded her. She smiled and drew in a deep, satisfying breath.

"The pond is that way." He pointed straight ahead. "We'll head there in a minute. First, I want to show you something."

"Aren't your sister and the girls waiting for us? We're already late." After their breakfast for two turned into a feast for six—not that she was complaining, because she wasn't. She'd enjoyed spending time with Mia's girls more than she would have expected. In fact, she'd rather liked the commotion of a family sitting down for a meal together, though she was hardly dressed for fishing so she'd asked Shane to stop at her place so she could change into jeans, a sweatshirt and sneakers. Mia and her daughters had headed straight here.

"They can wait a few more minutes. This won't take long." He grasped her hand in his and tugged her to the left.

They walked along the narrow dirt path for a while. Layla marveled at the quiet strength and gentleness of his grip and the sensation of the weight of his hand in hers. She enjoyed the peaceful tranquility and the beauty of the nature surrounding them. She couldn't remember the last time she felt this relaxed, comfortable.

"We're here," Shane said finally. "What do you think?" He gestured for her to precede him.

She stepped into the clearing. The sound struck her first. Water rushed over the edge of what had to be a ten foot tall natural rock wall into a small pool below.

Sunlight glinted through the surrounding trees creating a rainbow at the foot of the falls. "It's breathtaking."

Shane nodded. "Yeah. It is." A serene smile crossed his face. "It's the perfect place to just be."

Layla glanced up at him. "That's a good way of putting it."

"See the spot right there?" He pointed about ten feet in front of them where a thin stream of water jutted off the main pool. "The fishing is amazing right there."

"It is, is it? I thought you fished in the pond?"

"I do, especially when I take the girls, but I like coming here when I'm by myself."

"Your special place."

"Yes." He turned his attention to her. "This is where I'd wanted to bring you when I asked you to come fishing with me all those years ago."

"Really?" A burst of warmth flooded through her. "I thought you'd told me a group of people would be going."

"I'd planned to whisk you away when no one was looking. I was hoping for my first kiss." He released her hand and wrapped his arm around her and drew her in close.

He'd wanted his first kiss to be with her? Her heart sang. She looped her arms around his neck. "Maybe we can share that kiss now?" She nibbled at his bottom lip.

"I don't know." His arms tightened around her. "I'm not fourteen anymore." He grinned.

"I think we can still make it memorable." Layla pressed her lips to the hollow at the base of his neck and flicked her tongue over the sensitive spot. She delighted in the shiver that ran through him.

"You're off to a good start so far." His husky voice boosted her confidence.

"Only good? I guess I need to try harder." She angled his head down.

The depth of desire in his gaze stunned her. He pressed his body against her so that every inch of him contacted every inch of her. His lips crushed hers. The wanting inside her flashed to a white-hot need.

A torrent of emotions swept through her like fire devouring a dry forest. She'd never experienced anything like it before.

This man, this moment would be imprinted in her mind forevermore.

Layla wasn't sure how much time had passed when he finally eased away from her. Her mind kept spinning like the Tilt-A-Whirl at an amusement park.

"Definitely memorable." Shane grinned.

Layla burst out laughing. "Was it worth waiting for all these years?"

"Hell, yes."

"I'm so glad you brought me here today."

"Me, too." Shane waggled his brows.

Layla gazed up at him. "Maybe we could come back some time and fish here together."

"Yeah?" A boyish smile crossed his face.

"Absolutely." Layla grinned back.

"It'll be fun." He pinned her with that sexy smile she adored and she almost went weak in the knees.

"Speaking of which, how about we go and find the rest of your family, and you give me my first lesson."

"You've got it." Shane dropped his arm from her shoulder and grasped her hand in his.

Layla spotted Mia a few minutes later. Shane's nieces were running around the grassy area in front of the water.

Brooke came up to Shane and tagged him on the arm. "You're it." She took off running.

He handed her the two poles he'd carried from the car and raced off after the girls.

Layla laughed when he lifted Kiera in his arm and raced after Brooke and Aurora.

"So…" Mia slanted her gaze in Layla's direction. "Just friends, huh?" She let out a little chuckle.

Heat rose up her neck and flooded her cheeks. They were more than "friends," but what exactly, Layla couldn't say. "I can't put a label on what we are right now. It's too new."

"But you like him," Mia said. It wasn't a question.

It was more than like, which was absolutely unbelievable. They hardly knew each other.

"I'll take that silly grin on your face as a yes," Mia retorted.

"That's a pretty safe assumption," Layla confirmed. She couldn't stop smiling.

"He's a good guy." Mia gestured as Shane made his way toward where they stood, laughing while Kiera squirmed and wriggled in one arm and Brooke in the other.

"He definitely has a way with your girls."

"Yes, he does," Mia agreed. "He'd be a great dad someday."

Layla jerked her gaze to Mia. "What?" Her mouth gaped open.

"Just sayin'." Mia gave a satisfied smirk.

An image formed in her head of a little boy, with her smile and Shane's eyes. Layla froze. What was wrong with her? She shook her head to dislodge the image. Man, she was losing it.

Get a grip. Fast.

"Do you want kids someday?" Mia asked casually.

No. No matter what kind of image she had in mind, she couldn't let herself get distracted. She needed to focus on her career. *You need to work at it to stay at the top of your game, ma chérie.* Antoine's words echoed in her head. *Chez Antoine needs you. I need you. We won't have time for raising a family.*

Of course Antoine had never wanted children. He'd been too into himself for that. Yet another thing she hadn't realized before he'd cheated. Before he'd so coldly betrayed her trust.

But what did *she* want?

Keira's, Brooke's and Aurora's squeals filled the air. She glanced at Shane, and there it was again. That intense connection she'd only experienced with this man.

The laughter and joy on his face as he played with his nieces.

Layla smiled. "Maybe. Someday." She had time to decide. She was only twenty-nine.

"I win," Shane announced. He set each girl down

when he reached where she and Mia stood. "What do you say we get this fishing expedition started?"

"Yeah," Brooke said. She and her sisters ran toward an empty spot by the edge of the water.

Mia hurried after them.

"Ready?" Shane gestured toward the water.

She nodded. "You bet."

He slung an arm around her shoulder as they walked. "I'm glad you came today."

Her heart turned over. Layla smiled up at him. "Me, too."

Layla pulled into the parking lot at La Cabane de La Mer at eleven thirty the next morning. The restaurant might be closed on Mondays, but she still had things to take care of.

She noticed a car parked close to the building. Two women stood at the front entrance. Layla pulled into a nearby space and slid from her car.

The two women came toward her as she reached the stone walkway leading to the door.

"Layla." The stylishly dressed fiftysomething woman with a classic blunt-cut bob grasped Layla's hands in hers. "It's so good to see you."

"Jane." What was Shane's mother doing here? She closed her gaping mouth. "It's nice to see you, too."

Layla glanced from Jane to the other woman and back to Jane. "What can I do for you?"

"Mia's thirtieth birthday is coming up soon. We're interested in throwing a surprise party for her here. We stopped by to see if you have any of your private rooms available on—" Jane checked her calendar and rattled off the date. "But we can come back later. I didn't realize the restaurant is closed today."

"Yes," Layla agreed. "We're only open four days a week during the off-season."

"We can come back when you're open. I'm Piper Kavanaugh, Mia's younger sister." The woman extended her hand to Layla.

"I didn't know Mia had a younger sister." Shane had never mentioned it to her and neither had Mia. Layla shook her hand. "It's nice to meet you."

"Piper is home visiting for a couple of weeks, but I'm hoping to convince her to make her stay permanent." Jane aimed a conspiratorial wink in Layla's direction.

"Mother." Piper rolled her eyes skyward.

"Well, I am. I love having you home." Jane directed her attention to Layla. "When should we come back?"

"I don't mind showing you around now." She'd be out of her mind to turn away potential business, especially right now. Besides, this was Shane's mother. No way would she turn her away. She could take care of the few things she needed to do here after the women left. "Come with me." She gestured for Jane and Piper to follow her.

"Wonderful." Jane clapped her hands together.

Layla grabbed the keys from her pocket and unlocked the door. "Please, go ahead in." She stepped aside and allowed Jane and Piper to enter. "I'll get the lights." She flicked the switch to the left of the door. The entryway brightened.

Piper peered around the space. "This is lovely." She turned her attention to her mother. "No wonder you thought this would be the perfect place for Mia's party." To Layla she said, "She's been raving about this place since we started talking about surprising Mia."

"Well, it is fabulous." Jane winked and smiled a wide grin.

A warm pressure filled her chest. Layla smiled back. "Give me a minute to get the rest of the lights." She stepped around the small wall dividing the bar area from the entrance. Moving quickly, she strode to the back wall, opened the electrical box hidden behind the bar and flipped the circuit breakers.

Layla returned to the front entrance and motioned for Jane and Piper to follow her. She crossed to the dining room. "Here we are." She gestured her hand around the room.

Piper stepped into the glass and metal structure. "Oh, my." She hurried to the windows overlooking the ocean. "We came here once or twice when your grandfather ran his restaurant, but I don't remember the view being so... Well, spectacular doesn't cover it."

Yes. She couldn't, no wouldn't, lose this place. Layla moved to Piper's side and Jane followed. The three of them stood in silence watching the waves roll on shore.

"How many people are you thinking?" she asked after a few minutes.

"Between fifteen and twenty. Right?" Piper shot Jane a questioning glance.

"That sounds about right. The guest list is small," Jane confirmed.

"That gives us a few options." Layla smiled. "Why don't we take a walk and I'll show you what's available." She led them to the smallest of her private dining rooms. The former library when Grandma and Grandpa used the home as a private residence. "This room can accommodate up to twenty people."

"I love all the wood in the room." Jane gestured to the long wall lined with oak bookshelves and the oak paneling and trim throughout the space.

"Yes," Piper agreed. "It's lovely, but it feels a bit cramped with the massive table in the center of the room."

"Okay. I have a bigger room next door." She walked down the hall and opened the double doors. "This room seats about thirty people. We can remove a few of the smaller tables if you'd like a different setup."

Piper gazed around the room. "It's lovely, but… Do you have anything with a view of the ocean? Mia would love that."

"Just the main dining room. I can book a few tables in there. It's fine with such a small group," Layla answered.

"We wouldn't want to disturb your other patrons," Jane said. "The kids can get a little rowdy sometimes."

"What about upstairs?" Piper asked. "Is there a room up there with an ocean view?"

"I'm afraid not." Layla gestured for Jane and Piper to precede her into the hall. Once in the hallway, she closed the door and turned to face them. "The upstairs isn't part of the restaurant."

"That's right. Your grandfather used to live up there." Jane pointed to the ceiling. "When he ran his place."

Layla nodded. "It's empty right now. I'm considering renting it out. As commercial space, since no one can live there." She needed to ping her attorney again since he'd yet to respond.

Jane cocked her head to the side, as if considering. "How much space is up there?"

"About three thousand square feet. Why?" Layla asked.

Jane glanced at Piper. "That's enough space for what you want to do."

"Mom—"

"Oh, come on. It couldn't hurt to look." To Layla, Jane said, "Could we see it? Piper might be interested in renting."

"What for?" Layla asked.

Jane beamed a proud smile. "Piper wants to open an art gallery."

"Sounds interesting," she said.

"I've been thinking about it for a while, and with the annual art festival here in New Suffolk every summer pulling in some big names, now might be the time. If I can find the right space."

Layla nodded. "Sounds like you've done your research."

"Can we please see it?" Jane's eyes danced with excitement.

"Sure. Follow me." Layla walked past the front entrance to a large room on the right, across from the bar. She opened the curved oak paneled doors and stepped inside.

"Oh, my." Piper's wide gaze locked on the sweeping staircase on the left side of the room. "It's stunning." She walked across the gleaming wood floors and stroked her hand over the oak banister.

"Look at the medallion surrounding the chandelier." Jane pointed to the ornate plaster decorative rondure in the center of the ceiling.

"There are three ways to access the upstairs. This staircase." Layla gestured to where Piper stood, her hand still resting on the carved wood handrail. "The back staircase, located in the kitchen, and the elevator."

"Where's the elevator?" Jane peered around the room. "I don't see it."

Layla walked to the door to the right of the staircase and opened it. "Right here."

Piper nodded and came to stand by Layla's side. "I like the accessibility. That's a plus in my book." She summoned the car and stepped inside when the metal doors opened. "I can't wait to see what's upstairs."

Layla gestured for Jane to precede her into the car. Moments later the doors opened on the second floor. "We'll exit through the door on the opposite side of the car." Layla pointed behind her. Stepping into the hall she added, "This way." She pointed to her left.

"Oh, this is gorgeous." Piper gasped as she stepped into the spacious living room. "All of this open space. And the natural light. It's magnificent."

Layla nodded. "My grandfather removed what used to be the master bedroom and two spare rooms on the left side of the house to create this space."

Jane walked to the French doors that opened onto

a massive deck that ran the width of the house. "I can see why. Look at this view." She pointed to the afternoon sun glinting off the sea below.

Piper moved to Jane's side. "Spectacular. What other rooms are up here?"

"There's a kitchen to your right, two bedrooms and a full bath that overlook the front yard," Layla answered.

Piper turned toward the front of the house. "Mind if I look?"

"Not at all." Layla followed Piper. She opened the bedroom door on the left side of the house. "This is the spare bedroom. Obviously, you wouldn't use it as such. Maybe you could set up an office or something like that."

Piper nodded, a thoughtful expression on her face. She walked back into the living room. "I love it. It's perfect. Show me where to sign on the dotted line."

Layla chuckled. "We'll have to do a credit check on you first."

"Of course." Piper nodded. "That's no problem. I would expect as much. You'd be okay with me using this space as an art gallery?"

Layla studied her. "Yes." She couldn't think of a reason against leasing out the space for such a business. "I'm curious. Why this space? Have you looked at other places?"

"I checked out the vacant store on Main Street, but the space isn't big enough. And the barn that's for sale on the outskirts of town, but that needs too many renovations to make it work for me and it's too far from town.

"You have the square footage I'm looking for in a

great location." Piper looked Layla in the eye. "I'm serious about my new venture. I'm happy to share my business plan with you and prove I have the funds required to get my business off the ground."

Layla nodded. "Let's get the paperwork started, and we'll see where this goes."

"She can have the space?" Jane couldn't hide her excitement at the prospect.

Layla directed her attention to Piper. "If everything checks out and we can agree on the lease, then I think we can strike a deal."

Piper grinned. "Let me know what you need from me and I'll get it to you right away. I'm eager to get started."

"I'll do that."

"All righty." Jane smiled. "Now that we've settled that, let's talk about Mia's birthday party. Could we do it up here?" Hope gleamed in her eyes.

"Sure," Layla said. She wanted the business. "We can bring up a few tables and chairs from the restaurant and set the room up however you guys like best. Do you want to discuss menu options now?"

The sound of chimes filled the air.

"That's me." Jane pulled her phone from her purse and glanced at the screen. "It's work. I need to take this."

"No problem," Layla responded. "We're done here."

Jane walked to the far side of the room.

"I'll send you some menu options this afternoon," she told Piper.

"Perfect. And make sure to keep the date open. You're on the guest list for this event."

Layla smiled. "Thank you. I can't wait."

Jane returned to where she and Piper stood. "I've got to get back to the office and get some work done. Are you ready to go?" she asked Piper.

"Sure." Piper headed toward the stairs and she and Jane followed.

"Let me know what you need from me to start the lease process going," Piper said when they reached the front entrance.

Layla smiled a mile-wide grin. "I will."

"I'm looking forward to our new venture." Piper extended her hand to Layla.

Layla fastened her palm to Piper's. "Me, too."

"Bye," Jane and Piper said in unison as they strode out the door.

"Take care." Layla let out a loud squeal as she locked the front entrance. She couldn't believe her luck. Who would have guessed she'd find someone interested in renting the upstairs so quickly? Not her, that's for sure. The rent Piper would pay would bring her that much closer to making her business loan current.

Layla grabbed her phone and sent a quick text to Shane.

That calls for a celebration, came his quick response. Let's do something fun tonight.

I can't wait, she texted back.

Chapter Eleven

"My, aren't we in a hurry." Duncan shot a speculative glance across the ambulance at Shane.

"Yes, as a matter of fact. I am." He checked the flashlight to make sure the batteries worked, and moved on to the oxygen tanks. The levels looked good. "I've got plans for tonight." He checked the pressure bandage stock. Full. Duncan must have replenished the bin already. The ambulance was now ready for the next call.

Shane jumped down onto the concrete floor. He glanced at his watch. "If I don't get going soon, I'm going to be late."

"Who's the lucky lady?"

He snorted and let loose a little chuckle. "Layla."

"Williams?" Duncan's stunned expression spoke volumes.

"Yes, Layla Williams. Don't look so surprised."

"Can't help it." Duncan gave a slight shrug of his shoulders. "I would never have pegged you as her type. You're a jeans and T-shirt kind of a guy and she's… sophisticated."

"So what?" Shane barked. "What are you trying to say?" *She's out of your league.*

No. Damn it. He and Layla got along great. He could talk to her, and she listened. Really listened.

His mind raced back to the evening of that horrible accident with the kid. She'd wanted to make sure *he* was all right. Her care and compassion *for him* had floored him.

And the sex… *Phenomenal.*

"Whoa." Duncan stepped back and raised his hands in front of him. "I'm surprised, that's all."

Hell. Maybe he'd overreacted. *No maybe about it.* "Forget it." He pointed his thumb over his shoulder at the ambulance. "Everything is restocked."

Shane shoved his hands in his pockets. "I've gotta get going. See ya later." He exited the ambulance bay and headed toward the locker room.

What was up with him just now? Why had he gotten upset with Duncan?

Because he liked Layla. A lot.

You're worried Duncan might be right.

Layla bit her lip as she stared at her reflection in the mirror that hung on the back of her bedroom door. "What do you think?" she asked the woman standing next to her.

Elle let loose a wolf whistle. "That dress is awesome." She plucked at the sparkly clingy black fabric that clung to Layla like a second skin.

"Thanks." Layla grinned. "My sister bought it for me for my birthday. At a boutique in Manhattan."

"How are things between you?" Elle asked.

She'd mentioned her predicament with Zara to Elle after the last phone call with her sister in the hope that Elle might have some insight. Unfortunately, Elle couldn't offer any guidance.

She'd thought about asking Mia, but decided against it since she's Shane's sister.

"Not really great. I think we're just going to have to sit down with each other and hash it all out." Something she'd do when she'd finished sorting things out with the restaurant, even if worse came to worst and she lost her place.

Layla shook off the thought. She moved to her grandmother's wood vanity and sat on the dainty stool.

Shane wanted to celebrate tonight. She'd accomplished a lot in a short amount of time. She'd made the March payment. She was making the extra money required—barely, but she'd take it. Not to mention there was more than a good chance his sister would rent her space. Piper's credit check passed with flying colors this afternoon. A positive sign they were moving in the right direction.

She dusted the brush over the powder and highlighted her cheekbones with a touch of blush.

"It's perfect for a night of partying in Boston. Do you know where Shane is taking you?" Elle asked.

She shook her head and applied her favorite red lipstick. "He didn't say, but I'm assuming we'll eat at a restaurant downtown. Maybe grab a drink at a bar after." What else would they do? They were celebrating, after all.

Truth be told, Layla could care less where they went. She just wanted to be with Shane.

Elle shifted her weight and leaned back against the wall. "I wish they'd open something like that here in New Suffolk. There's nothing fancy or upscale, other than your place."

"Thank goodness." Layla winked. "Less competition." She spun away from the mirror and slipped her feet into her strappy black stiletto heels. Standing, she did a little twirl.

Elle winked. "Shane is going to love it."

"He'd better."

She and Elle burst out laughing.

Her cell dinged. Layla grabbed it off the dresser. She scanned her fingerprint to unlock the screen and read Shane's incoming text.

On my way over to your place now.

She glanced at Elle. "He'll be here in a few minutes."

"That's my cue to leave. Have fun." Elle gave her a quick hug and left.

She picked up her clutch purse and stuck her phone inside. Walking into her living room, she strode to the closet.

At the loud knock, she switched directions and

headed to the door. Anticipation hummed and buzzed inside her. She yanked open the door.

Shane's mouth fell open.

So did hers. "Oh, crap."

"Layla." Shane stared at her. He couldn't help it. Why was she dressed as if they were heading out for a night on the town? *Because you said let's celebrate.* He'd been thinking pizza, beer and a few games at the Bowl-A-Rama, but she'd thought differently. Like the polar opposite.

I would have never pegged you as her type. Duncan's words from earlier this evening came rushing back to him. *You're a jeans and T-shirt kind of guy.* Shane glanced at his attire. He swallowed hard to clear the sudden lump in his throat. Duncan had been right about that.

No. The lack of communication was his bad, not hers. Not a problem. He could pivot. *A fancy dinner it is.* They'd start with drinks at an upscale bar in the city. He might be a jeans and T-shirt kind of guy, but he could clean up when an occasion called for such measures.

"You look gorgeous." He leaned in and kissed her.

"Thanks, but I'm feeling a bit overdressed."

Right. They'd have to stop at his place first.

Layla motioned for him to enter her apartment. "I get the feeling we're not on the same page for this evening."

"I'm sorry. That's on me. I'll change and we can head downtown for dinner."

She chuckled. "What was your original plan?"

"Pizza and beer at the Bowl-A-Rama." Heat flooded his cheeks.

"Bowling…" Surprise flickered in her gaze. "Okay. I'll change and we can leave."

"No." He shook his head. "You don't have to do that. We can stop at my house and—"

"It's fine." She flashed a warm smile and brushed her sweet lips against his.

Shane sighed. How could he be addicted to her kisses in such a short period of time? "Are you sure?"

Layla grinned. "I'm absolutely positive. I'll go change now."

They arrived at the Bowl-A-Rama fifteen minutes later.

A full moon glowed and stars twinkled like party lights in the clear night sky.

"It's a beautiful evening." Layla inhaled a deep breath and blew it out.

"It's a little cold, if you ask me." Shane grasped her palm and linked their hands together as they walked toward the entrance.

"Yes, but warmer weather is coming." Layla grinned at him. "Spring is almost here."

"Speaking of spring." Shane stopped and turned to face her. His insides jumped and jittered. Lord, why was he this nervous about asking her to go to the gala with him?

You're afraid she'll agree to accompany you and not show at the last minute like she did all those years ago, his fourteen-year-old self jeered.

That was delusional thinking. They weren't kids anymore. The Layla he'd gotten to know these past few weeks wouldn't do such a thing. Would she?

No, damn it.

"Will you be my date for the gala?" Layla's words came out in a rush.

His mouth fell open. He couldn't help it. Her question could not have surprised him more. Layla could be a bit shy sometimes. He wouldn't have expected her to ask him. "Yes." Shane grinned. He needn't have worried. She wanted him to attend the gala with her as much as he wanted her to come with him. "I'd love to."

"Great." Layla's face filled with happiness.

Shane started walking again. He was pretty sure he sported a happy grin.

He pulled the door open when they arrived at the front entrance and gestured for Layla to precede him. "Okay if we eat first?" he asked once he'd stepped inside.

"Sounds great. We can have a beer while we wait for our pizza."

"Perfect." His type of woman, for sure. "Lead the way."

Layla stuck her arm through his crooked arm and they walked to the Lava Lounge.

Shane pulled out the chair at one of the empty tables and gestured for Layla to sit. She did. He grabbed the chair next to her.

"So, I have a serious question for you." Layla gazed at him, a solemn expression on her lovely face.

"What's that?" He eyed her curiously.

"Are you an anchovy man?" She burst out laughing.

The sweet sound wrapped around him like a wisp of soft silk. "Nope. I don't like them at all, so you'll have to contain them to your half if you do."

"Nah." She waved off the notion. "I'm not a fan either, but I can go for pretty much anything else." Layla held up her pointer finger, and added, "Except pineapple. Not that I don't like pineapple, just not on my pizza."

Shane linked his hand with hers. He wanted the contact. "I believe we're on the same page." It was then he noticed the man sitting alone at the bar.

"Hey, what's up?" Layla asked. "Why are you frowning?"

"That's Cooper Turner at the bar."

Layla stared at the man who sat alone with a dejected expression on his face. "He looks like hell."

Shane nodded. "Yeah."

She placed her palm on top of his hand. "Go talk to him. Make sure he's all right."

He'd been thinking the same thing. "You don't mind? We're supposed to be out on a date."

Layla arched a brow. "Of course I don't. He looks like he needs a friend."

There was that care and compassion he admired once again. Shane hopped up from his chair. He kissed her. "Thanks. I'll be right back."

"You're welcome."

He crossed the room and dropped down in the empty seat on Cooper's right side. "Fancy meeting you here."

Cooper glanced over. He dragged a hand through his already disheveled hair. "Hey."

Shane studied his friend. He couldn't miss the bloodshot eyes and drawn expression on his face. "What's up? You don't look so good."

"I haven't slept in more than twenty-four hours."

Shane's brows furrowed. "Why? What's kept you up? Your family—" He sucked in a deep breath.

Cooper shook his head. "They're all fine."

"Then what gives?"

"Turns out you and my brother were right about women after all."

Shane remembered the conversation they'd had at Donahue's. Was that really only three weeks ago? Maybe he'd been too harsh when he'd said those things. Too cynical? Spending time with Layla had… He still wasn't looking for forever, but things were great right now.

He glanced at her, and she smiled at him. A flood of warmth rushed through him. What was he going to do about her?

He couldn't think about it now. He needed to focus on other important matters. His job still hung in the balance—he'd be right back where he started if she couldn't save her business.

Returning his attention to Cooper, he said, "About that."

Coop held up a hand. "I know. I know. I should have listened to you. And Levi, too. He was right about Rachel after all."

"Your girlfriend?" he asked. "What was Levi right about?"

"Rachel is *not* my girlfriend. Not anymore." Cooper shook his head.

Shane clapped Cooper on the shoulder. "I'm sorry. What happened? You two seemed perfect for each other."

"Yeah." Cooper scrubbed his hands over his face. "You think you know someone."

Shane's gaze jerked to Layla. Her actions over the last couple of weeks had blown all of his preconceptions of her out of the water, but how well did he really know her?

"And they turn on you. Morph into someone you can't recognize."

Melinda's face popped into his head. His heart squeezed. No, damn it. He wouldn't think about the past.

Shane sucked in a deep breath, but he couldn't banish his inner demons. No matter how hard he tried.

The doorbell rang. Layla glanced at her watch. Shane was early. Her pulse jumped and skittered. "Coming."

She shoved the pan containing the Monte Cristo sandwiches she'd prepared aside and raced to her door.

Layla tripped on the throw rug in the living room in her haste but caught herself before she face-planted on the floor. God, what was wrong with her tonight? You'd think she hadn't seen Shane in months the way she was rushing around. The reality was, she'd seen him less than twelve hours ago.

She'd enjoyed bowling last night even with all her

gutter balls, but after the game… And again, this morning… Layla grinned. *Spectacular.*

The bell sounded again. "I'll be right there." She walked the rest of the way and opened the door. "Come on—" Her jaw dropped. "What are you two doing here?"

"Don't look so excited to see us." Elle handed her a bottle of wine. "We thought it would be more fun if we all watched the What's Cooking segment together." She stepped inside.

"Yes," Abby agreed and followed behind Elle. "Mia wanted to come, but she's busy with her girls."

Abby cocked her head toward the coffee table where Layla had set two wine goblets and a chilled bottle of Pinot Grigio. "Goblets? A chilled bottle of vino. I'd say Layla is planning to watch the What's Cooking segment with someone else."

"Maybe." Warmth flooded her cheeks. "Okay, yes. Shane will be here any minute."

Elle snorted and turned to Abby. "Look at that silly grin plastered on her face."

"Yep." Abby nodded sagely. "She's got it real bad for the hot EMT."

Layla protested, "I do not."

"Oh, yeah. You definitely do." Elle smirked.

They were right, and that terrified and thrilled her at the same time. Terrified because this thing between them was developing fast. She'd never experienced this connection, this sense of exhilaration when she was with him, this…rightness before. Certainly not with Antoine.

Thrilled because she and Shane fit together like Brie and baguettes, or butter and croissants. It wouldn't take much to fall hard for this man. *Back to the terrifying part again.*

The doorbell rang.

"That'll be Lover Boy." Abby winked. She grasped Elle's arm. "We need to leave."

Layla rushed to the door and yanked it open. Her pulse skyrocketed. Good heavens, dressed in his snug-fitting jeans and a burnt-orange button-down shirt, the man looked delectable. Yes, she had it bad for Shane, all right. "Hi."

He gave her his trademark sexy grin. "Hey."

"Hi, Shane." Abby pushed by her and rushed into the hall. She dragged Elle with her.

"Bye, Shane." Elle waved.

"Ladies." His brows furrowed. "Don't rush off on my account."

Layla nodded. "You guys are more than welcome to stay."

"That's great." Elle tugged Abby back through her door.

"Please, come in." She moved aside to allow Shane entry.

Shane stepped in and closed the door. His gaze roamed over her. "Hi."

"Hi." She caught a glimpse of Elle and Abby watching them from the couch. She stepped to the side to block their view.

"Spoilsport," Elle grumbled.

Shane chuckled and brushed a chaste kiss over her lips.

"How was your day?" she asked.

"Slow. Just one call. Nothing too serious." He shrugged off his bomber jacket and draped it on the back of a chair.

"Have a seat." She jerked her head toward the living room. "I'll grab dinner." She leveled a glance at Elle and Abby because she knew they were listening. "There's enough for all of us."

Abby bumped her fist to Elle's.

"I hope you don't mind being my guinea pig again," she said to Shane. "I'm trying something a little different with my Monte Cristo sandwiches and I wanted your opinion."

"Count me in anytime," Shane said. "You know I'm always happy to be your taste tester. Can I pour you some wine?"

"I'll get two extra glasses from the kitchen," Elle said.

Shane chuckled. "All right. Red or white?" he asked Abby.

"Red, please."

"Me, too," Elle called from the kitchen.

"I'll have white," she said. She hurried into the kitchen. Plating each sandwich, she dusted the tops with powdered sugar and placed a dollop of raspberry jam to the side.

"Hurry, Layla. The What's Cooking segment is on right after this commercial," Shane called from the couch.

"Be right there." She grasped two plates in each hand and walked into the living room. After presenting dishes to both Elle and Abby, she sat next to Shane and handed him a plate.

Placing hers in her lap, she used her knife to spread the jam on the tops of each half of her sandwich.

Shane copied her.

"I'm so excited. I can't wait to see the segment," Abby said.

"Me, too." He bit into his sandwich, closed his eyes and let out a satisfied groan. "Oh God, that is so good!"

Layla grinned a mile wide. She adored his genuine enthusiasm when it came to her cooking. "Glad you're enjoying it."

"Thanks for cooking dinner."

"You're welcome." She leaned over and placed a quick kiss on his lips.

The commercial ended and the news anchor appeared on the television. "It's time for What's Cooking," he said.

"I can't wait to hear what's on the menu today," the female anchor said.

"What do you have for us, Cal?" the male anchor asked.

Cal Conway appeared on the screen. He stood in the open area just beyond the entrance to her restaurant.

She sucked in a deep breath and blew it out slowly. "Here we go."

"You're in for a real treat today," Cal said.

Layla gripped Shane's arm and squeezed. "That's a good start."

Shane grinned. "It is."

"I'm in New Suffolk today," Cal continued. "At The Sea Shack."

Oh, my God. Layla gasped.

"Did…he just call your restaurant by the wrong name?" Abby asked, sounding confused.

"Yes!" She threw her arms up in the air and nearly sent her plate flying. "It's *La Cabane de La Mer*. For God's sake," she yelled at the TV.

Shane shook his head. "I don't understand. Why would he call your place The Sea Shack? How would he come up with that?"

Layla dragged a shaky hand through her hair and told him about her conversation with Cal during the segment shoot. "I mean, he asked me for the translation, which is fine, but I can't believe he screwed up the name. How could he have done that? What am I going to do?"

Shane looked as frustrated as she felt. "We can alter the metadata on your website so that if someone googles *the sea shack* your restaurant name will come up. It's not a perfect solution, but it will help at least until they can correct their error." He took her hand. "Come on. Let's at least see what they thought about the food."

She returned her attention to the television. The video of her chopping vegetables appeared on-screen and Cal said something about her being a top chef from Paris. He must have researched her because she couldn't recall that fact coming up when he'd interviewed her. More images of the other dishes she'd prepared during Cal's visit appeared, but he made no commentary on what they were.

"Those look great," Shane said.

"Yes, but how are people supposed to know what they are? I don't understand why he cut everything we talked about."

The scene cut to the dining room filled with people. The camera zoomed in on Elle and Abby.

"Ooh, there we are." Elle grinned.

"You were there?" Layla couldn't recall seeing them the day the crew filmed the segment. Then again, she'd been busy with other things that day.

"Of course we were," Abby said. "We told you, we've got your back."

Yes. They had. "Thanks, guys. It means a lot that you came out to support me."

"We love your place." Elle flashed a big smile.

"Yes," Abby agreed. "The food is terrific."

A rush of warmth flooded through her at their kind words.

The scene cut back to Cal who sat at a table in the dining room.

"But this is the best thing on the menu," Cal said.

The camera zoomed in on the burger she'd made him. Cal picked up the burger in both hands and the camera now focused on his face. He bit into it.

"Oh yeah." Cal closed his eyes. He sighed and a huge smile crossed his face. "I tell you, folks, I've never had a burger like this in my career."

The segment ended and the news anchor appeared on-screen again. "And there you have it. Head to The

Sea Shack in New Suffolk for the best burgers in the state."

"Correction," the other anchor added. "There seems to be a mistake regarding the restaurant name. It's La Cabane de La Mer." She rattled off the address.

"Well—" Layla rubbed her fingers against her throbbing temples. She'd counted on this review to increase her customer base. That wasn't going to happen. She was right back where she and Shane started a few short weeks ago.

"We'll leave you two alone." Abby and Elle hurried to the door.

"Bye, ladies," Shane said.

The door clicked shut. Silence thundered around the room. A burst of hysterical laughter bubbled up and erupted from her, and she turned to Shane. "What the hell am I going to do now?" she asked, feeling more lost than she had when she'd first returned from Paris.

Shane could see the confusion and worse, the panic in Layla's gaze. Quickly, he grabbed the remote and turned off the TV, then wrapped an arm around Layla and pulled her against him. "It's going to be okay."

She stared at him as if he'd grown horns.

Hell, even he couldn't believe that sentiment. How could he when, despite loving the food, that critic had basically undercut everything she'd worked so hard to achieve over the past few weeks?

She pulled away, frustration edging the hysteria from her tone. "How can you even say that when he not only failed to talk about all the new dishes, but the only item he praised isn't on the menu at all? I'm not a burger joint. I don't want to run a burger joint. That was never my dream, damn it."

Shane felt desperate. "Layla, we can't give up just because of this." If La Cabane de La Mer went under...

No, he couldn't lose his job. Being a paramedic was what he wanted to do.

Layla straightened her shoulders and held her head up high. She looked him in the eyes. "You're right. Everything will be fine. I'll make sure of it."

Shane prayed they'd find a way to make her words come true.

Chapter Twelve

"It's packed out there. Again." Olivia walked into the kitchen at La Cabane de La Mer on Thursday afternoon.

Layla glanced up from the prep station. "Seven days in a row now." It was hard to believe a little more than a week had passed since the What's Cooking segment had aired. It had served its purpose. Maybe not quite the way she'd imagined, but she'd be thankful for the extra money coming in.

She set the last of the burgers she was making on the counter and blew out a breath. The strands of hair that had come loose from her bun fluttered in the air for a moment before they settled on her skin again and stuck to the perspiration on the side of her face. "What are you doing here this early? Dinner preparation doesn't start until four thirty."

Olivia let out a hearty chuckle. "It is four thirty."

Layla's mouth gaped open. "Already?" She'd been going nonstop since she'd arrived this morning.

"Any specials tonight I need to get started on?" Olivia asked.

"No." Layla shook her head. None of her traditional specialties had sold well since the What's Cooking segment had aired. Most people came in for the burgers, especially during lunch.

An idea came to mind after she'd talked with a couple who'd come to her restaurant after seeing the cooking segment. They'd ordered the burger Cal had touted, but had questions on the rest of the items on her menu. The woman had wanted the chicken dish shown on the segment, but couldn't figure out which chicken dish it was from the names printed on the menu. It occurred to her that most people wouldn't know coq au vin from chicken Provençale.

She'd revamped the menu last evening. Now La Cabane de La Mer offered classic American dishes with a French twist. "I ordered some filets of beef yesterday and added them to the menu. You can serve them with the brandy-laced sauce in the pot on the back burner."

"You mean steak Diane?" Olivia asked.

"Yes, but I'm serving the Sea Shack Filet," the name she'd printed on the menu, "with traditional mashed potatoes and some grilled asparagus. There are options for an herbed butter sauce or a béarnaise sauce as well. The dish can also be prepared with no sauces if that's what a customer wants."

Olivia stared at her, a wild-eyed expression on her face.

Layla could relate, but she wasn't selling out. Not really. Changes were necessary if she wanted to keep the restaurant in business. And that's what she wanted. *No doubt about it.*

She'd contacted her webmistress right after the What's Cooking segment had aired instructing them to add The Sea Shack, in parentheses below the name.

Her coq au vin was now listed on the menu as Chicken in Red Wine Sauce. The ingredients were the same. She prepared the dish the same way, but used the loose English translation instead of the French name. She'd done the same with her boeuf bourguignon, now renamed Hearty Beef Stew. And she'd sold out of every ounce today.

The biggest change was adding "the best burger in the state" to her repertoire on a permanent basis. The Sea Shack Burger, as it was now known, held a prominent position on the menu.

Layla laughed to herself. She'd gone through a week's worth of ground beef and sausage the first day after the segment had aired. Thank goodness she'd been able to quadruple her order and the butcher had delivered the next morning. That reminded her, she'd need to order more with the weekend coming.

Yes, she'd done what needed to be done in order to keep her restaurant in business.

Her cell buzzed. "Can you take over this for me?" She pointed at the burgers sitting on the counter. "They all need to be cooked medium rare."

"Sure." Olivia nodded.

"Thanks. The last of the fried potatoes are in the

warming tray. Have Luis make more if needed. He'll need to make the mashed potatoes, too." Layla hurried to the sink and washed her hands. Her cell had stopped ringing, but she'd call whoever back. She dried her hands. Snapping her fingers, she added, "Have Luis throw in a few baked potatoes. Some customers might prefer them to mashed."

Olivia's brows rose, but she nodded.

Done. At last. Layla stepped out of the kitchen and into the hall. She rolled her shoulders and neck and let out a weary sigh. Every muscle hurt. She couldn't wait to get home, pour herself a glass of wine and soak in a hot bath.

"Oh, there you are." Sam approached carrying an empty tray.

"What's up?" she asked.

"The gentleman at table four would like to speak with you."

Damn. Her shoulders slumped. *Not done yet after all.* "Of course." The vino and bubbles would have to wait a bit longer.

Layla straightened her toque and strode into the dining room. A smile curved on her face when she noticed who sat at table four. "Shane."

"Hey, gorgeous."

She looked down at her chef's coat and spotted a red stain on her right pocket. Splatter from the tomatoes she'd sliced earlier? Or maybe it came from the beef stew? She couldn't say.

Her feet throbbed. Back ached. "I don't know about that."

"I do. You're beautiful." He stood and landed a fast kiss on her startled lips.

Her heart did a little flip. "Thank you. What are you doing here? I thought you were working again tonight?" They'd been constantly missing each other these past few days, with his shifts starting as her day at the restaurant ended.

A slow smile formed on his face. "One of the guys asked me to switch and I jumped at the chance."

"Oh, yeah? Why is that?"

"Why do you think?" He winked at her.

Because you missed me as much as I missed you? No. That was ridiculous. She couldn't afford to fall for him. Someone else was bound to catch his eye.

Shane isn't Antoine. He wouldn't cheat on her, would he? *Stop it.* He hadn't given her any reason to suspect such behavior from him. Looking back, she should have seen the signs of Antoine's infidelity, but he'd always had a reason for disappearing from the restaurant in the middle of the afternoon, and she'd chalked up his sudden interest in getting fit to wanting to be in his best shape for their wedding day.

"Everything okay?" Shane's voice pulled her from her morose thoughts.

What was wrong with her tonight? This gorgeous, sinfully sexy man had jumped at the chance to spend time with her. She needed to get over her insecurities. Layla pasted a smile in place. "Everything is fine."

"Well, then…" He aimed a sexy grin at her. "Got any plans tonight?"

Layla whispered in his ear, "You and me in my soaker tub."

Heat sizzled in Shane's gaze. "How about a hot tub instead?"

"I don't have a hot tub."

"I do. It's out on the back deck."

Layla couldn't remember seeing it the night they'd watched the sun set. Then again, she wasn't paying much attention to what was on his deck. She'd been too busy enjoying the view. "Works for me. Now, what can I get for you this evening, monsieur? Perhaps our new Sea Shack Filet?"

Shane's brows furrowed. "More menu changes?"

"Just catering to my customer base. Like you said the evening you reviewed my business financials, this is New Suffolk not Paris," Layla whispered. And the natives seemed to like the changes she'd implemented thus far.

Whatever it takes to keep this place. She'd do it. She'd succeed no matter what.

Shane peered around the restaurant. Same decor, same tables, dishes, flatware, glasses. The waitstaff wore the same uniforms they'd worn since Layla had opened the place. So how could the vibe of this place have changed? Sure, she'd Americanized some of the items on the menu. Shane glanced at the parchment in his hand again. Not some of the menu. She'd Americanized the entire offering. Yes, the changes she'd implemented would save her restaurant. He was sure of that, but at what cost?

Layla wanted to own a French restaurant and this place was morphing into... He wasn't sure what this place was, but it was most definitely not what she'd dreamed of owning. Of that he was sure. Which meant what moving forward?

He didn't know. Why that worried him, he couldn't say. He only knew that it did.

The next evening, Layla placed another invoice on top of the pile on the corner of her desk. Leaning against the soft leather of her chair, she closed her eyes and enjoyed the relative silence her office afforded. The sounds from the dining room seeped in and Layla sighed. She turned to her computer and pulled up her produce supplier's website.

Her cell buzzed. She glanced at the incoming number and smiled. Grabbing her phone, she connected the call. "Hi, Shane."

"Just wanted to let you know I'll pick you up in five minutes."

"Great. I'll be ready to go when you arrive." She hoped this evening together would be a repeat of last night. Especially what came after the long soak in Shane's hot tub.

"See you soon." Shane disconnected the call.

Layla grinned as she returned her attention to the task at hand.

"Knock, knock, knock," a familiar female voice called a few minutes later.

She jerked her gaze to the woman standing in the doorway. *Oh, my gosh.* "What are you doing here?"

"I know you've wanted to talk for a while, but I haven't been ready. I am now."

Layla smiled. "I'm happy to see you."

"I'm sorry." Zara threw her arms around Layla.

"Me, too." She held her sister tight.

"I see the restaurant is doing better." She released Layla and gestured behind her in the direction of the dining room. "Honestly, I thought we were doomed."

"Yes. The changes I've made are paying off." She'd meet the deadline the private lender had stipulated—just.

Relief flooded Zara's delicate features. "I was hoping that was the case when I saw all the extra money being deposited into the account." Zara shot her a quizzical look. "How did you turn things around?"

Layla walked over and sat in the seat she'd vacated moments ago. "I got some expert advice." Lucky for her Shane had needed La Cabane de La Mer to survive so she could host the EMS spring gala fundraiser. The gala would go on as planned.

Zara's brows furrowed. "How did you manage that? Business consultants don't come cheap."

Right. Layla opened her mouth to respond and closed it abruptly when Shane appeared in the doorway. Oh, my, the man looked delicious. Her heart beat a little faster. *Can you say sucker for a man in uniform?*

"No, they don't," Shane agreed.

"And who might you be?" Zara asked in a flirty voice.

Layla's hands curled into tight fists. She wanted to tell her sister to back off her man.

Whoa. Where had *that* thought come from?

She gave herself a mental shake. God, what was wrong with her this evening? Layla sucked in a deep breath and released it. "You remember Shane Kavanaugh, don't you?"

Zara's brows furrowed. She stared at Shane for long moments. "I think I'd remember you if we'd ever met."

Shane let out a soft chuckle. "We've met before, but it's been a while. I worked at the country club during those summers you and your family used to visit New Suffolk."

"Oh, my." Zara's eyes widened. "Yes, yes. I remember now." She let her gaze slide over him from head to toes. "You certainly turned out quite handsome."

Shane's smile made Layla's pulse go wild. "Well, thank you very much."

Was Shane flirting with Zara? Were they flirting with each other?

No, damn it. Paranoid much? Thanks, Antoine.

Shane walked over and quickly kissed her surprised lips, and propped his long lean frame against the file cabinet next to her desk. "It's nice to see you again, Zara. When did you get into town?"

"Just a few minutes ago. I wanted to surprise Layla."

"You surprised me all right." Layla nodded. "A good surprise. I've missed you."

Zara gave a warm smile. "I've missed you, too. Is it okay if I stay with you tonight?"

"Um…" She glanced at Shane. So much for their repeat of last night. "Sure." What else could she say?

"So, what were you two talking about when I walked in?" Shane asked.

"How well the restaurant is doing," Layla said.

"Yes," Zara agreed. "You were going to tell me about this business consultant you engaged."

"You're looking at him." Shane pointed a thumb at himself.

"You?" Zara's brows furrowed. "Don't take this the wrong way, but what does an EMT know about restaurant finances? At least I assume you're an EMT based on the uniform you are wearing. My grandfather had a similar one when he worked for the New Suffolk regional EMS."

"Shane spent more than five years on Wall Street fixing failing businesses. He's a whiz at finances."

"Yeah, right. That's me." Shane gave a soft chuckle.

Zara turned a thousand-megawatt smile on Shane. "Oh really? Well, isn't that interesting. Very interesting, indeed," she muttered under her breath. "Lucky for us you came along."

Another knock drew Layla's attention to the doorway once more. "What's up, Olivia? Is there a problem in the kitchen?"

"We've had to 86 the coq au vin—seems it's really popular tonight. Do you want to offer anything on special to make up for that?"

Layla stood. "Let me check the cooler and see what we can offer as a substitute." She turned her attention to Shane and Zara. "Excuse me for a few minutes, please."

"Go ahead." Shane smiled and gestured toward the

door. "Zara and I will get reacquainted while you're gone."

Now why did that worry her?

Shane flashed what he hoped was a pleasant smile. He'd never liked Zara or the other rich snobs she'd hung around with at the country club. Their servant boy attitude had turned him off from the beginning.

Layla wasn't like them. Never had been. He couldn't see it back then. He'd lumped the lot of them together without getting to know them personally. He needed to rectify that now. *For Layla.* "So…"

"So…" Zara chuckled. "What's there to do around here for fun?"

"Depends on what you consider fun. It's the beginning of April. That's still the off-season. The beach bars don't open until Memorial Day. Same with the day cruises and fishing expeditions, but the movie theater is open and so is the Bowl-A-Rama."

"Bowling?" Zara doubled over with laughter. "Yeah, right. That's a good one."

What had she expected? This wasn't Manhattan. *Thank God.*

"Wait. You're serious?" she asked, taking in his expression.

He nodded. "Try it. You might find you like it."

"Oh, I've tried it. Grandpa used to take Layla and me when we came to visit." Zara let loose a chuckle. "Layla hates bowling."

"What?" His brows drew together. She seemed to

have a good time with him when they went to the Bowl-A-Rama last week.

"With a passion," Zara added. "She sucks at it."

He remembered all her gutter balls. Still, she'd laughed them off. He could have sworn she'd enjoyed herself that evening.

She never told you that she hated it. But she'd dismissed the idea when he'd suggested they play a few games the other day.

"Looks like the three of us will have to go to Boston tonight," Zara said. "We can grab dinner at the brasserie. I can't remember the name of the place, but I'm sure Layla will remember. We've been there a couple of times before. Oh, and there's a great nightclub. We used to go all the time when I was here last fall."

"Hey, guys. I'm back." Layla walked into her office.

An image of the party girl from last week popped into his head.

"Everything okay?" Zara asked.

"Yes. Olivia is working on a substitute chicken dish now."

Zara smiled a wide grin. "Great. That means we can head out."

Layla's brows drew together. "I'm game to go out for a bite to eat. Olivia will cover the dinner service here, but where are we going?"

"To that restaurant in Boston we used to go to when I was here last year. You remember? It was right after you opened La Cabane de La Mer. We used to go clubbing after we ate," Zara announced.

"Right." Layla laughed. "Yes. Of course."

"Just like old times." Zara winked.

"Sounds like fun," Layla enthused. A wide smile crossed her face.

She wanted to go clubbing, just like Zara had told him.

Different worlds. Shane's shoulders sank.

He tried to silence the voice in his head but couldn't.

Layla woke. Bright sunlight flooded the living room. It was morning already? Hadn't they just gone to bed a few minutes ago?

They'd arrived home from their night out in Boston after two in the morning. She'd given Zara her bedroom and slept on the pull-out sofa bed. Layla rubbed her lower back. *Comfy my ass!* The salesman had lied. That's for sure.

Layla reached for Shane. She craved the sense of pleasure…contentment…rightness she'd found waking in his arms each morning. She'd never experienced that with another man before.

Her arm hit the pillow. *Right.* He'd decided to stay at his place. He'd wanted to give her some alone time with her sister.

She glanced at the clock on the wall. Nine thirty. That was almost eight hours of sleep. Why was she still tired? Worse, why did every muscle in her legs hurt? Oh, yes. That would be from hours of dancing on stiletto heels. Stupid move on her part when she'd been on her feet all day. Why had she agreed to Zara's plans?

"Just like old times." Zara's words echoed in her head. Layla didn't want the old times. She'd changed

over the last nine months. She wanted poker night with
the girls, pool and beers at Donahue's... *Shane*. Yes,
she wanted to see where this thing with him might lead.

Should have gone bowling last night. It would have
been more fun. Layla threw back the blanket and
grinned.

She swung her legs over the edge of the mattress and
stood. She padded down the hall toward the bathroom,
jumping when the bedroom door opened and banged
with a loud thud against the bedroom wall.

"Don't go in there." Zara raced into the hall. "I need
to get ready and I'm running late."

"Where are you going?" she asked.

Zara didn't answer. She disappeared inside the bathroom and slammed the door shut.

Where could her sister be going? She knocked on the
door. "Don't be too long. I have to get ready for work."

"Okay. No problem," came Zara's muffled reply.

"I thought we could do breakfast before I have to
head over to La Cabane de La Mer."

The door opened a crack and Zara peeked out.
"Can't. I already have plans."

Layla's brows drew together. "With who?" It wasn't
like her sister knew many people here in New Suffolk
anymore.

"A friend." Zara slammed the door shut again.

"Fine." Layla rolled her eyes skyward and walked
to the kitchen. She needed caffeine. Now. She busied
herself making coffee.

Mug in hand, she moved to the sofa and grabbed

her phone from the coffee table. Setting her mug down, she texted Shane.

Breakfast at the Coffee Palace this morning? Layla typed and hit Send.

She waited. A few minutes went by before he responded, Wish I could, but something came up this morning that I need to take care of.

Maybe tomorrow, she typed and added a frown emoji.

Definitely.

Will I see you later today? Layla hit Send.

A thumbs-up emoji appeared on her screen along with the message, Stop by my place after you're done at the restaurant.

Layla smiled. Okay, she replied.

The bathroom door creaked open.

"It's all yours." Zara raced across the hall with a fluffy white towel wrapped around her.

"Thanks." Layla rose and strode into the kitchen. She swallowed the last of her coffee, rinsed the mug and set it in the sink. She walked back to her bedroom to grab her clothes, but found the door locked. She lifted her fist to knock but decided against it when she heard the sound of Zara's hair dryer.

She padded across the hall and closed the bathroom door.

Silence greeted her fifteen minutes later when she emerged. "Zara?"

No answer came.

Layla walked into her bedroom and found the room empty. She continued into the living room. Zara wasn't there, either. "She must have left," she muttered as she returned to her room. Why she hadn't said goodbye, Layla couldn't say.

Layla dressed in her whites and headed out twenty minutes later.

She passed the town green, marveling at the crocuses beginning to bloom in some of the flower beds. Spring was well on its way and she couldn't wait for the warmer weather.

She glanced in the window at the clothing on display at the trendy boutique and the trinkets at the souvenir shop. Layla stopped short in front of the local diner when she noticed Zara sitting at one of the booths with Shane.

Her breath hitched. What were they doing together?

Executing a one-hundred-and-eighty-degree turn, Layla strode to the entrance and stepped inside.

Shane noticed her. Panic flooded his features before he could mask the emotion with a smile and a wave.

Layla swallowed hard as she made her way through the crowded, noisy waiting area to the table where her sister and Shane sat.

"Come join us, please." Shane slid out of the booth. He dropped an awkward kiss on her cheek before gesturing for her to slide in.

Layla sat, and Shane joined her.

"What are you doing here?" Zara's tone sounded accusing.

Layla tilted her head and sent her sister an appraising glance. "Funny. I was just going to ask you the same question. I thought you had plans to meet a friend?"

"I did." Zara's eyes bugged out. "Do." She coughed and sputtered. "I mean I do. Have plans."

She glanced from Zara to Shane and back at Zara again. "You're meeting Shane for breakfast?"

"What? You think I planned to meet Shane? Here at the diner?" Zara let out a nervous laugh. "Now why would you say that?"

Shane heaved out a weary sigh. "It's a logical conclusion to draw. I am sitting here with you."

"Oh. Right. Um..." Zara aimed a winsome smile at her. "I'm waiting for my friend. Shane was kind enough to join me so I didn't have to wait alone."

Okay. That made sense, but why not say as much from the beginning? Why was her sister acting all kinds of weird? Shane, too, although, not as weird as her sister.

The server appeared and placed a breakfast sandwich in front of Shane and a plate of scrambled eggs, bacon and toast in front of Zara.

Layla's brows drew together. "You ordered before the friend you're meeting has arrived? That doesn't make any sense."

"Well... I'm hungry." Zara nodded her head. "Yes. I'm famished. I couldn't wait a moment more." She stabbed her fork into the eggs and shoved them in her mouth.

"What is up with you?" Layla threw her hands up in the air as she stared at her sister who continued to shovel eggs into her mouth.

"Nothing." Zara set down her fork and shook her head. "I told you. I'm hungry. That's all."

"Okay." Layla arched a brow. "If you say so."

"I do," Zara said. She plucked up her toast and took a bite.

Definitely weird. Layla turned her attention to Shane. "What about you? Did you finish your errands already, or did you stop in for breakfast first before you head out?"

"He stopped here to grab something to go." Zara stuffed a piece of bacon in her mouth. "Right, Shane? Isn't that what you told me? You wanted to grab something to eat before you took care of a few things." She returned her attention to Layla and nodded her head vigorously. "That's what he said when I got here. And that's when I asked if he'd join me so I wouldn't have to wait alone. For my friend."

Shane glared at Zara. "But you don't need me anymore now that Layla is here. Why don't you fill her in on what you told me?" He swallowed the last of his sandwich and wiped his mouth with a napkin. He leaned over and kissed Layla again. "I'll call you later." He dropped twenty-five dollars on the table. "Breakfast is on me. Have a great day, ladies." He strode to the exit.

"I should get going, too." Zara slid from the booth. "I'll catch up with you later." She disappeared outside before Layla could protest.

Layla stared at the empty booth. What was going on with Shane and her sister?

She needed to find out. Fast.

Chapter Thirteen

Shane stood at the kitchen sink, rinsing the brush he'd used to paint the trim.

The doorbell sounded. He frowned. He wasn't expecting anyone. He only had a couple of hours off between shifts today. Except...damn. He'd forgotten to text Layla and let her know he needed to cover a shift tonight for one of the guys out sick.

His heart beat a little quicker at the thought of seeing her again, especially after he'd left the diner so abruptly this morning.

Shane shook his head. He should have insisted Zara tell Layla about their meeting. He'd assumed she'd join them after Zara had asked him last night to meet her for breakfast today because she needed some advice regarding La Cabane de La Mer's finances. Layla's text this morning asking him if he wanted to join her for breakfast had confused him. He'd been about to text her back saying as much when his phone rang. Zara had called him to let him know she'd be late and asked him not to tell Layla about their meeting. He hadn't liked keeping their meeting a secret, but had agreed after Zara told him it was urgent she speak with him first.

"Hold on a minute," Shane called. "I'll be right there."

Shane turned off the faucet. He shook the water from the paintbrush and set it on the edge of the sink. After wiping his hands on the dish towel that hung on the oven handle, he noticed the paint stains on his T-shirt and stripped it off as he walked. He'd toss it in the laundry after he let Layla in. Opening the door he said, "Sorry for making you wait. I was—" His brows furrowed into a deep V. "Zara, what are you doing here?"

Zara's mouth dropped open. She cleared her throat and aimed a hesitant smile at him. "I hope you don't mind me stopping by. I wanted to finish our conversation from earlier this morning."

"What more is there to discuss?" he asked. "Haven't you told Layla you don't want to manage her restaurant's finances?" He'd left them alone this morning to give them time to talk.

"There was something more I wanted to ask you before I talked to my sister. Please. Hear me out. If you care anything for Layla…"

"Okay." The word popped out of his mouth before he had a chance to think about the implication. Yeah. It was true he did care for her. A lot more than he should, but he couldn't think about that right now. He stepped away from the door and gestured for her to come in. "I only have a few minutes." He needed to be back at the EMS building in less than thirty minutes.

Zara nodded and stepped inside. "Thanks. This won't take long."

"So, what more did you need to tell me?" Had something more happened since the last time he'd reviewed the restaurant's financial statements?

Zara straightened her shoulders. "I want you to take over for me."

Shane blinked. He couldn't have heard her right. "Say that again."

Her chuckle annoyed the heck out of him. "Oh, come on. You're the perfect replacement for me. A whiz with finances, by your own admission. I know you already have a full-time job that you love, and I'm not asking you to give that up. You wouldn't need to. Now that we're in the black again, thanks to you, of course, it would only require a few hours a week to keep us that way."

More than a few, that's for sure, but...he'd enjoyed the challenge of helping Layla turn things around with her business over the last few weeks. Truth be told he missed that excitement. The sense of accomplishment when something broken became whole again. Not that he wanted to return to Wall Street. No. He loved his EMT job. He wouldn't give up his dream of becoming a paramedic. Not for anything.

If he managed Layla's restaurant finances he would

have the excitement, the challenge he missed. He and Layla could—

What the hell was he thinking? "No. That's not going to work long term." He and Layla were a "for now" thing. Definitely not a forever thing.

What happened when things ended between them?

His gut twisted at the thought.

Shane scrubbed his hands over his face. What was going on inside him? He'd never felt these emotions for any woman. Not even his ex-wife.

He wasn't in love with Layla. Was he?

Honestly, he wasn't sure. All he knew was that he didn't want things to end with her. That scared the hell out of him.

"Please, Shane. You're my only hope." Zara's voice snapped him from his thoughts.

He shook his head. "Have you even run this by Layla yet?"

A pained expression crossed Zara's face. "I wanted your agreement before I broached the subject. My quitting will be less of a blow if I can assure her I have a replacement. Someone she can trust to do better for her than I did."

"No way. Layla deserves better than you going behind her back. You need to be up-front with her. She needs to have a say in this."

"But, Shane. I—"

He held up his hand to stop any further protest from her. "It's not up for debate. Talk to your sister. You owe her that much." Only then could they have a conversation on the subject.

Zara's phone pinged.

"That's Layla. I need to take this. She's been calling me all day. I'll just be a minute." Zara grabbed her cell from her pocket and answered. "Hey, sis. What's up?"

Shane glanced at his watch. "I need to get ready for work." He started for the stairs and stopped when the front bell rang. Shane opened the door. His mouth dropped open. "Layla."

"Yes, it's me." She shoved her phone in her pocket and marched inside. "What is going on with you two?" Her angry gaze flicked to her sister and back to him.

He wouldn't panic. He'd done nothing wrong, but given her experience with Antoine... He could only imagine what she was thinking. "This is not what it looks like. There's nothing going on here. I swear."

He needed Layla to believe him. If she didn't...

Acid burned in his gut.

Layla's stomach heaved. No, damn it. Her sister wouldn't betray her, and Shane...

He's not Antoine. Shane didn't strike her as the cheating type. There had to be a reasonable explanation as to why her sister had come to Shane's house and why he was standing there half-dressed.

Please, please, please.

Shane shrugged on the T-shirt he held in his hand. A sense of déjà vu hit her. She recalled the first time she came here, when Shane reviewed her restaurant's finances. All of those glorious muscles on display when he'd opened the door bare chested.

Paint splatter covered his shirt. There was a spot on

his chin she hadn't noticed when she'd first arrived. The scent of fresh paint filled the house.

He'd obviously been painting right before she'd arrived. She released the breath she'd been holding.

Shane wasn't cheating on her, but something was up. "If it's not what it looks like, what is it?" Layla darted her gaze from Shane to her sister.

Zara's guilty expression spoke volumes.

"Let's start with you, *sis*. First, your bizarre behavior this morning, then you avoid my calls all day, and when you finally answer... You told me you were out and about town, but you're here. Why would you lie to me?"

"I didn't, exactly." Zara twisted her hands together.

Shane threw his arms in the air. "For God's sake, would you just tell her what's going on?"

Zara looked like a deer in headlights. "I don't want to manage La Cabane de La Mer's finances anymore," she blurted. "The restaurant is your dream, not mine."

Layla couldn't move. Couldn't breathe. Zara wanted out? A dozen questions flooded her mind.

"Did you hear me?" Zara asked. Concern etched her gaze.

"Yes." Layla gave herself a mental shake. "Is this the reason for your bizarre behavior today?"

Zara cringed. "I'd planned on telling you when I came to your office last night, then Shane arrived and you told me how he helped you and I thought he'd be perfect for the job."

"The two of you went behind my back." Her voice dripped with accusation.

"No." Shane shook his head. "I wouldn't do that to you."

"He's right," Zara said. "Shane thought you'd be joining us this morning. I asked him not to mention anything to you after you texted him to see if he was free for breakfast. *I* wanted to ask him if he'd take over managing the restaurant finances before I spoke to you. I thought you'd take the news better if I found a replacement before I told you I wanted out. You know how I avoid conflict at all costs."

Yes, and it was part of why they'd ended up in trouble. Layla couldn't dump all the blame for what happened with the restaurant on her sister. She bore a chunk of the responsibility for their financial problems, too, but things could have been different if Zara had told her they were having problems making payments instead of avoiding the issue and hoping it would resolve itself.

"I asked him to meet me this morning, only you showed up before I could mention my proposal. That's why I came here."

Her mind spun faster than her commercial mixer switched on the highest speed, but one clear thought came through. She needed someone to manage her restaurant's finances. Someone she could count on. Someone who knew what they were doing. *Someone I trust.* Shane fit the bill on all accounts, but would he do it? She turned to him. "What did you say?"

Zara cut in before he could answer. "You mean besides reading me the riot act about not leveling with you, and giving you a say in this?"

Yay, Shane! He had her back, and that meant the world to her. "Does that mean you'll do it?" She held her breath and crossed her fingers that he'd say yes.

"Is that what you want?" He wouldn't want her to feel obligated just because her sister desired an easy out.

"Yes." Layla shot him a hopeful look. "You're the perfect person for the job. I have faith in you." Her expression grew serious. "And you...you had faith in me when I didn't know what to do."

She believed in him. His heart started hammering. How lucky was he to receive such a generous gift?

Damned lucky, that's for sure.

"Are *you* sure you want to take this on given everything else you have on your plate?" Concern etched Layla's gaze. "You don't have to. I won't be offended if you decide it's too much right now."

She was right. He had a lot going on right now. His job. Renovating his home. They consumed most of his time but... The more he thought about it, the more he wanted to do this, and not on a temporary basis. Shane grinned. "Of course I want to do it."

"You're hired. Name your salary. Within reason, please." Layla threw her arms around him and kissed him hard.

"Perfect." Zara rushed over and threw her arms around him and Layla.

He thought about the party girl, the lousy bowler, the woman who'd gone fishing with him and the fun-loving woman who'd painted a stripe down the front of his sweatshirt.

Layla was perfect for him. In every way.

He'd be lying if he said that didn't scare the heck out of him.

"Are you ready?" Layla glanced across her desk at her sister who sat in one of the chairs opposite her.

Zara grinned. "Are you kidding? You've dragged me out of bed at the crack of dawn on a cold Monday morning for this. Of course, I'm ready."

"First of all, it's almost noon. Not o'dark-thirty. Second, this is Massachusetts, and it's still the beginning of April, not July thirtieth. Mornings can be cold. You should have dressed warmer."

Zara rolled her eyes. "Regardless, let's get on with this. I need to head back to the city as soon as we're done."

"All right." Layla logged into her account. "Here we go."

Zara jumped up from her seat and raced around to Layla's side of the desk. "I want to see you do this."

"Okay." She keyed in the dollar amount and hit Send. "The loan is now current. A day before the deadline." They wouldn't lose the restaurant. Relief flooded through her with the force of a tidal wave crashing on shore during a turbulent storm.

Zara threw her arms around her. "You did it. You should be proud of yourself."

"I am." She'd learned a lot over the last few weeks and she wouldn't make the same mistakes twice.

"Well, I'm off now."

Layla rose. "I'll walk you out." She gestured to Zara to precede her out of the office.

"See you later." Zara gave her one last hug and stepped through the main entrance of the restaurant.

"Drive safe." Layla waved as Zara strode to her car. "Give my love to Mom and Dad the next time you see them."

"Will do."

Layla stood in the front entrance to La Cabane de La Mer until Zara's car disappeared. She was about to close and lock the door when a black F-150 truck pulled into the parking lot. A thrill of excitement trickled down her spine when Shane hopped out and strode toward her. What was it about this man that made her insides go all soft and mushy when he walked into a room?

"Hi." Was that breathy voice hers? Yeah, it was. Boy, she really did have it bad for him.

His brows furrowed as he came through the door. He dropped a quick kiss on her lips and asked, "Where is your sign for the restaurant? It's missing from the post out front."

Layla drew in a deep breath and pasted what she hoped passed for a genuine smile on her face. "John, from Show Me A Sign, came out this morning to pick it up. He's going to add The Sea Shack under La Cabane de La Mer. In smaller letters, of course."

Shane couldn't look more surprised. "I know we talked about adding the translation to your website..." He didn't finish his sentence.

"Yes. People really resonated with the name so I decided to add it to the sign out front to make sure people knew La Cabane de La Mer and The Sea Shack were the same place."

"Are you okay with that?" Shane's compassionate gaze was almost her undoing.

"Of course." She blinked back her tears before he could see the evidence of her lie. Her authentic French bistro was quickly morphing into an ordinary restaurant. Her worst fear come true.

No, damn it. She needed to look on the bright side of things. She had much to be thankful for. The private lender wouldn't foreclose on her. She wouldn't have to face her grandfather and tell him she'd lost his beloved property.

Everything would be fine. It would. *It has to be.*

"So why did you want me to stop by?" Shane asked.

Layla let out a breath, relieved at the change of subject. "I have great news."

"Oh, yeah?" He waggled his brows.

She sighed. Lord, the man was utterly adorable.

"What's your news?" he asked.

"Come with me, and I'll tell you." She grasped his hand and led him into the bar. "Have a seat." She pointed to the chair on the end closest to where they stood.

"Yes, ma'am." He gave her a jaunty salute and sat in the seat she designated. "Okay. What's up?"

Layla stepped behind the bar and leaned her elbows on the glossy surface. "A few weeks ago, you walked into the restaurant and found me here, in this spot.

I was distraught and thought I'd lost everything that mattered to me."

"Layla—" he began.

She held up a hand to stop what he might say. "Please. Let me finish."

He nodded and she continued.

"You helped me turn things around, and you stuck with me when I initially resisted making the changes I *needed* to make." She leaned down and grasped a bottle of wine she'd set on the shelf under the bar.

"I'm happy to report that as of today," Layla paused for effect. "The loan is current."

Shane's gaze widened. "You made the payment?"

"Yes." Layla was pretty sure she was grinning from ear to ear. "Zara and I made it this morning." Thank goodness because the Spring Gala was only four days away. "I wanted a clean slate when you took over the finances. You still want to do that, right?"

"I do." He joined her behind the bar. "We need to celebrate."

"I agree." She presented the bottle of wine to him. "Remember this?"

Shane smiled and let out a low whistle. "Château Lafite Rothschild Pauillac. How could I forget?"

She'd always remember the evening he'd turned her world upside down. He was just what she'd needed, and she couldn't be happier. "It's the last bottle. We agreed to break it open."

He winced. "Bad choice of words."

Layla laughed as she recalled that evening Shane had stopped by the restaurant. The night Zara had broken the news of her impending financial ruin. He scared the daylights out of her. She'd knocked the bottles and sent them flying. They'd crashed on the tile floor, spilling more than a thousand dollars' worth of wine everywhere.

Layla grinned. She'd come a long way since then. "Right." She placed the bottle on the bar top and uncorked it. Setting the corkscrew aside, she placed two long-stem glasses beside the bottle and filled them halfway.

She handed a glass to Shane and grabbed the other for herself.

"To us." Shane raised his glass. "We make a great team, don't we?"

Layla clinked her glass to his and sipped. "Yes." Her heart did a crazy little flip. "We do."

"Get out of here." Olivia escorted Layla to the door of the kitchen at La Cabane de La Mer. "You're supposed to be attending the gala, not working here in the kitchen."

"But I need to check—" she began, but Olivia cut in.

"You don't need to check on anything. The meals have been served. Go join the others and have fun. We've got this." Olivia gestured to the others in the kitchen. "Enjoy yourself. You deserve it."

"Are you sure?" she asked.

Olivia rolled her eyes skyward. "Go." She pointed to the door.

"Okay, okay." Layla pushed the swinging door open and ran straight into Shane.

"Here you are." He pulled her against him. "I thought you'd never finish."

Layla luxuriated in the feel of his strong arms wrapped around her. A sense of rightness flooded through her, of coming home after too long away. "I'm sorry. I wanted to make sure everything went off without a hitch."

Shane let out a low chuckle and she shivered. "You achieved that. With flying colors." He gestured behind him to the smiling people milling about in the lobby and beyond. "The food was phenomenal. Everyone is raving about it."

"I'm so glad everyone enjoyed it." Layla smiled, pleased.

"Of course they did. How could you believe otherwise? You're an extraordinary chef." He nuzzled the hollow behind her ear. "But you've been in the kitchen all night. I've been waiting to see you."

She let out a little sigh. "One of my waitstaff came down with the flu. I filled in until one of the other waiters could come in."

He eased her away from him but didn't let her go. "You look amazing." His heated gaze trailed down her body and back up again. "Red is definitely your color. This material…" He brushed his fingers over the short clingy skirt of her dress. "Amazing."

Shivers ran down her spine. "I'm glad you like it." *So worth the cost.* "You clean up pretty nice yourself." Layla swallowed hard. He'd removed his black suit jacket and loosened his bow tie. His white dress shirt couldn't disguise his strong shoulders and sculpted chest, and the way his black trousers fit his lean, narrow hips... *Oh, my.*

Shane let out a low growl and tugged her against him again. His hard body pressed against her from head to toes. He lowered his head and ravaged her mouth, leaving her breathless. "I've been dying to do that all night. Days actually."

She sucked in some much-needed air and steadied herself.

He pressed featherlight kisses down the column of her neck and her knees nearly gave way. "Between all the hours you've put in here at the restaurant, cooking and setting up for tonight, and my EMS shifts, we haven't seen each other in four days."

Since they'd celebrated her making the loan current. Layla basked in the press of his warm body against hers.

He cupped her face and caressed her cheeks with his thumbs. "I missed you."

His admission sent her spirit soaring. Unable to contain the happiness surging through her, Layla launched herself into his arms. "I missed you, too."

"Good." Shane flashed a wicked smile. He jerked his head toward the front of the restaurant. "Come dance with me. I want to hold you in my arms for a while."

Yes, please. "I'd love to." Every inch of her sizzled with anticipation.

Shane held Layla's hand as they walked into the La Cabane de La Mer's bar. He needed the contact with her. Lord, what was wrong with him tonight? You'd think they hadn't seen each other in months, not days. He couldn't explain it, or the fact that she'd occupied his mind all day, every day. He'd even dreamed about her. Not sexy, erotic dreams. Those he'd have understood. No, these visions were of everyday life together. He and Layla picking out new kitchen appliances, the two of them cooking in his new kitchen together. The two of them watching movies together on the couch in front of a blazing fire. What was up with that?

"Where is everyone?" Layla's words broke into his musings.

He peered around the space. A disc jockey was set up in the right corner of the room, but the space was otherwise empty. "They're probably in the private dining rooms bidding on the silent auction items, or in the main dining room eating dessert." He could care less where the others were. "Come here." He grinned and drew Layla into his embrace.

She melted into his arms, pressing so close it was hard to tell where he ended and she began. A deep sense of satisfaction filled him. Yes. This was what he needed. What he craved.

Layla moved even closer, if that was possible, and rested her head on his shoulder. He marveled at how perfectly her body fit with his.

A sense of peace and contentment filled him as they moved together to the slow, sensual beat of the music.

All of a sudden, Layla froze. Every muscle pressed against him turned rigid. She jerked her head up and gaped.

"What's wrong?" His gaze searched her shocked

expression. A shiver ran through him at the anger he saw in her gaze.

She untwined her arms from around his neck and stepped back.

"What are *you* doing here?" Disbelief thundered through every word she spoke.

Shane turned his gaze to the man who stood in front of them. He hadn't heard anyone approach.

"Layla, *mon amour*," the man said.

"I am not your love, Antoine." Her lips tightened into a thin line.

Antoine? Shane's gaze went wide. As in her ex-fiancé? The man looked like some kind of Greek god. He laid an arm around her shoulder and pulled her back into the crook of his arm.

"What do you want?" Layla asked.

Shane wondered the same thing.

Antoine spoke, but Shane couldn't understand what he said.

"Speak in English," Layla shot at him. "We're not in Paris anymore."

"Very well." Antoine sounded like a man trying to appease a child. "I wanted to speak with you." He shot Shane a derisive look, and turned his attention back to Layla. "Somewhere private, *s'il vous plaît*."

Hands on hips, Layla glared at him. "You can't just waltz into my life after more than a year and make demands."

Antoine's face grew serious. "Please. It's important. This can't wait."

Indecision flickered across her features.

Shane gave her a gentle squeeze. "You don't have to do this," he whispered.

She smiled and kissed his cheek. "It's okay. I'll only be a moment."

Antoine glared at Shane. "This will take more than a few minutes." He muttered something more in French.

"Antoine." Layla glared at her ex.

Shane didn't need the translation to understand he'd been insulted. It took every ounce of control not to lunge at him, but he managed it. For Layla's sake.

Layla kissed him again. "I'll be right back. I promise."

His nerves skittered, and a sliver of doubt knifed through his heart.

Layla's heart raced as she strode down the hall to her office. At least it was better than the initial nausea swirling in her stomach when she'd first heard Antoine's voice.

What was he doing here?

He wants me back. It was the only explanation she could come up with for why he'd made the long trip from Paris to New Suffolk.

Could it be true? Her pulse pounded, mind whirled at the possibility.

"*Mon amour.* Please…"

She rounded on him. How dare he call her that after what he'd done to her? How dare he waltz into her restaurant as if what happened all those months ago never happened. As if he hadn't shredded her heart to pieces.

"I told you not to call me that."

He held up two hands as if he were surrendering. "Of course. I'm sorry." He aimed a sinfully sexy smile at her.

She sucked in a deep, calming breath and blew it out slowly.

"We'll talk in here." Layla walked through her office door and stepped aside to allow Antoine entry. "Please have a seat." She gestured to the chairs that stood in front of her desk.

Layla closed the door and sat in her chair behind her desk. She leaned back and tried to relax. Pinning what she hoped was a neutral expression on her face, she asked, "So, what was it you wanted to speak with me about?"

Antoine jumped up and raced around to her side of the desk. He knelt down on one knee and grasped her hands in his. "I want you back, Layla." He gazed lovingly into her eyes. "I've been miserable without you. I've missed you more than I thought possible."

"Antoine…" Her breath hitched.

"I've learned my lesson, *mon amour*. I can't live without you. Please forgive me."

Layla swallowed hard. How long had she secretly wished for this? Months if she were honest. Being without him in the early days… It had felt like a piece of her had died.

An image of Antoine and the blonde bombshell in bed flooded her brain. Her stomach heaved. "How can I trust you?"

He gave an endearing smile. "I am reformed. I love

you. We can take things slow. I want you back, Layla. In my personal life as well as my professional life."

Her brows furrowed. "You want me to come back and work for you at Chez Antoine?"

"But, of course. I should never have fired you. It was…childish of me." He heaved a dramatic sigh. "I was angry, and I allowed that anger to get the better of me. Can you forgive me?"

"I can't. My restaurant." She'd finally made the loan current.

"*Mon amour.* You are a three-Michelin-star chef."

Not anymore. Maybe never again. Her heart sank.

"You deserve so much more than a place like…like The Sea Shack." Antoine couldn't hide his distain. He pulled her to her feet. "You deserve to cook in the best gourmet French bistro in Paris."

It was what she'd always wanted. Wasn't it?

Good grief, what was she thinking? "I can't just shut this place down." Layla gestured about the space. "I used the mansion as collateral. I'll lose it if I can't pay off the loan. I'm not willing to do that."

Antoine's brows furrowed. "How much do you owe?"

Layla named the amount.

"That is nothing. I will pay for it. Anything to get you back."

Her jaw nearly hit the ground. "You're willing to pay off my loan?"

"You deserve it." He kissed her hand. "All you have to do is say yes and all your dreams will come true."

All her dreams… Yes, once upon a time they'd been her greatest desires. And now…

An image of Shane's handsome face filled her mind. "What do you say, *mon amour*? Will you come back to Paris with me?"

Chapter Fourteen

Shane paced back and forth in the hall outside Layla's office. He should probably wait in the dining room, but he couldn't. He needed to know what Antoine wanted. *One way or the other.* Nausea swirled in his gut.

"Mon amour." Antoine's muffled words of endearment drifted into the hallway.

His hands curled into tight fists. He couldn't understand the rest of what Antoine said since he spoke in French, but there was no mistaking that phrase, or the silence from Layla. She'd been adamant about Antoine not calling her his love before they'd gone into the office but now…

Why was he getting upset? It wasn't as if he was in love with Layla. *Love doesn't last.* They were having fun together. That was all. It didn't matter what Mr. Suave and Sophisticated said or did.

Yeah, right!

"Hey, Wall Street." Duncan clapped a hand on Shane's shoulder. "Have you seen Layla? I'm heading out and just wanted to say thanks for everything. The gala turned out great."

"Yeah, it did. She's in her office."

The office door opened. Antoine and Layla stood together.

Antoine said something, in French, of course, and Shane couldn't understand. He walked into the hall where he and Duncan stood and he smirked.

Shane wanted to smack the arrogant grin from Antoine's face.

Antoine turned back to Layla. "Until tomorrow." He blew a kiss.

Shane's gut twisted as Antoine strode away.

Layla turned her attention to Duncan. She gave a nervous smile. "What's up?"

"Ah…" Duncan looked at him and back at Layla.

Shane could only imagine what he was thinking.

"I just wanted to tell you what a great job you did. Everything was outstanding."

"Um… Thanks. I'm glad you enjoyed yourself."

Duncan turned to him. "Well, I'm leaving now. I'm on shift in fifteen minutes. Take care." He gave a wave that included both him and Layla and walked away.

"So…" Shane jammed his hands in his pockets. He wished he could lean against the door frame and adopt a casual stance, but he couldn't. "What did your ex want?" It didn't take a genius to figure out what Antoine wanted. He wanted Layla, but Shane wanted to hear that from her.

Layla blew out a breath. "He wants me back. He wants me to come back to Paris, to run the restaurant with him."

Shane almost doubled over from the verbal blow. He'd hoped against hope he'd been wrong, but he wasn't. He sucked in some much-needed air. "What do you want?"

"Shane, I—it's complicated." She sighed. "I need—"

His stomach plummeted. Was she actually considering reconciling with that idiot? With the guy who'd cheated on her before their wedding? Would she really leave New Suffolk and give up her life here, give up everything she'd worked for?

Give up everything they had together?

No, dammit. He cut her off. "Need time to think. I understand." No, he didn't. She should stay here. *Stay with me.* Shane stiffened.

He needed to get the hell out of here. Now. Before he said something they'd both regret.

Shane lifted the whiskey glass and sipped. As usual, Donahue's bar rocked on a Friday night. That was a good thing. The noise helped drown out the thoughts whirling in his head. He caught a glimpse of Duncan as he sidled up to the bar. "I'm fine." He hoped his words would stop Duncan from saying anything more.

"Really, cause you look like shit."

So much for hope. He didn't need this. "I thought you were supposed to work tonight. That's what you said right before you left the gala." Shane propped his hands on the glossy bar top and steepled his fingers. He stared at the shelves of liquor behind the bar.

"Had a short shift tonight. I'm already done. How many of them have you had?" Duncan nudged Shane's glass as he grabbed the chair next to him and sat.

Shane glared at Duncan. "Three maybe. I'm not counting." He glanced at his watch. One thirty in the morning. He'd left the gala early so he'd been here for more than four hours. "That's less than one an hour. You got a problem with that?" He wasn't drunk by any stretch of the imagination, but he'd Uber home just the same. He'd been on enough calls for DWIs to avoid the risk.

The bartender yelled out last call.

Duncan ordered a light beer. He turned to Shane. "So…"

He rolled his eyes. "You're not gonna leave me alone, are you?"

Duncan arched a brow. "If that's what you want, I'll drink my beer and head home."

Shane swallowed another sip of his drink. *Oh, what the hell.* "Layla's ex wants her back."

"How nice." Duncan snorted. "What does she want?" He lifted the glass the bartender set in front of him to his lips.

"I don't know." He dragged his fingers through his hair. "She needs time to *think*."

"I see." Duncan nodded. "Have you told her how you feel about her?"

Shane shrugged loosely. "I don't have feelings for her."

Duncan let out a low chuckle. "So that's how you're going to play it."

"You're the one who said you couldn't see us together."

"It doesn't matter what I think. How *you* feel is what matters." Duncan sipped his beer, then turned back to Shane. "For the record, I was wrong. You two are perfect for one another. Are you going to deny you're happy with her?"

"No." He'd never dreamed he could be as happy as he was when they were together. "But happiness doesn't last."

"What if it does when you're with the right person? What if Layla settles for this French shmuck because she doesn't know how you feel about her?"

"What if I tell her and she doesn't care?" He'd tried that before. Melinda hadn't given a rat's ass. He'd made a complete fool of himself.

Duncan shrugged. "You'll have to decide if that's a chance you're willing to take."

Shane sucked in some much-needed air. Could he risk everything and place his heart on the line again?

Layla woke the next morning with a pounding headache. She rolled over and glanced at the bedside clock. Ten. Any other day, she'd chide herself for sleeping the day away. She pulled the covers over her head. God, what was she going to do about Antoine?

The pounding continued and she realized someone was knocking on her apartment door. "Hold on a minute." She threw back the covers and slid out of bed.

Grabbing her robe, she slipped it on and made her way to the front door.

"Layla, are you there?" came a muffled voice from the hall.

"Elle?" Brows furrowed; Layla opened the door.

"Oh, good. You're here." Abby held on to a box of what Layla assumed was a selection of pastry from the Coffee Palace. She scooted past Layla and came into the living room.

Elle followed with a tray of coffees. Mia brought up the rear.

"Um…" Layla scrubbed her hands over her face. "Did I forget we were getting together this morning?"

"Nope." Elle set the tray on the coffee table and plopped down on the couch. She opened the box and plucked up a chocolate éclair.

"We wanted to see who tall, dark and handsome was?" Mia sat on the couch next to Elle.

Her brows drew into a deep V. "You mean Shane?"

Mia rolled her eyes. "Ew. No. The guy from last night. At the gala."

"The guy with the accent." Elle bit into the éclair.

"We were walking back to our table from the silent auction room when he came in. He interrupted your dance with my brother."

"Oh. I didn't realize you had seen him."

"Well, to be fair, he was hard to miss. Tall, dark, handsome." Elle squealed when Abby elbowed her in the ribs. She glared at Abby. "What'd you do that for?"

Abby shot her a menacing glance. "You're not helping."

"It's fine." Layla shrugged. Antoine was drop dead gorgeous. Elle was only stating the obvious.

"I think he's your ex." Abby sat in the club chair to the right of the couch. She grabbed one of the coffees and swallowed a sip.

"Is she right?" Elle asked.

"Yes. Antoine came to talk to me last night." She sat in the club chair opposite Abby and grabbed the last coffee. "He wants me back. Swears up and down that he's learned his lesson."

"Do you believe him?" Abby asked.

"He seemed sincere." She heaved out a sigh. "He wants me to go back to Paris with him in a few days."

"Hah." Elle snorted and shook her head. "That's easy for him to say. He's not the one giving up his life and moving halfway around the world—"

Layla arched a brow. "Tell me how you really feel, Elle."

"Okay. Okay. It's none of my business, but seriously, it's a huge thing he's asking of you. You've established a new life here. With good friends." Elle gestured to Mia, Abby and herself. "Let's not forget about how hard you've worked to make a success of your business. He wants you to give all of that up. That's not fair. He's the one who screwed things up."

"Sometimes life isn't fair." Mia jumped up and started pacing. "You know, I'd give anything if Kyle walked through my front door and told me he wanted me back." She turned her back on the group. "I know that sounds insane, but it's true nonetheless."

Layla's heart squeezed. She didn't know the circumstances behind Mia's split with her husband, but she could empathize with her situation. Mia wanted a second chance at living her dreams. Layla had been given one. So why hadn't she jumped at Antoine's offer?

"Let's say for a minute you went with him. What will you do with your restaurant?" Abby asked.

"Oh, my god. I totally forgot about that. What about the space my sister is supposed to rent from you for her art gallery?" Mia asked.

"That's still a go, although I won't be able to cater any of the events since I'll have to shut down the restaurant."

"How do you feel about that? Especially after you spent so much time and effort fixing things over the last month." Abby grabbed a chocolate croissant from the box and bit into it.

Sick to her stomach. That's how she felt. Her French bistro may have gone up in flames but The Sea Shack… It was all hers and she enjoyed creating the dishes she'd featured on the menu. Even the lunch menu. Sure, it might be more casual than she'd ever imagined…but she found it a creative challenge.

"Not great. That's part of the problem." How could she give up her place? *Her* place.

"See. That's what I'm talking about," Elle said. "It's not fair that you have to give up everything. Why can't Antoine come here, even if it's just for a short time?"

"What about Shane?" Mia asked.

Good question. She couldn't stop thinking about him.

"I know you two just started seeing each other, and it's none of my business, but—" Mia's voice trailed off.

"You don't want to see him hurt." Layla swallowed hard. The idea of hurting Shane… A painful lump formed in her chest making it hard to breathe.

"No. I don't. He doesn't deserve that. He's a good guy."

Not good. Shane was one of the *best* men she'd ever known. Kind, compassionate. He loved deeply and with all of his heart. His family, his community. Despite the wounds he'd suffered from the loss of his father. From his failed marriage.

His quiet strength kept her balanced.

Being with him made her happy. He was…everything she'd ever wanted, and more. She loved Shane.

She was one hundred percent in love with him. Layla grinned and jumped up from her chair and raced toward her bedroom.

"Where are you going?" Elle couldn't hide her surprise over Layla's sudden departure.

She stopped. "I'm going to get dressed. I need to speak to Antoine." To hell with waiting until noon. She'd go to his hotel now. Layla hurried into her room. She removed her robe and nightshirt and dressed in a pair of black jeans and a V-neck ecru cashmere sweater. After brushing her teeth and throwing her hair up into a messy bun, she walked back into the living room.

Three sets of eyes stared at her.

"What?" She grinned. She couldn't help it.

"Are you going to tell us what you're planning on saying to Antoine?" Abby asked.

"I don't love him anymore. I'm not going to Paris."

"Yay!" Elle, Mia and Abby cheered at once. They rushed over to where she stood.

"I'm so happy you're staying." Elle grinned.

"Me, too," Mia added.

"Me, three." Abby opened her arms. "This calls for a group hug."

"Yes. It does." Layla threw her arms around her friends and they all laughed. "I have to get going. I'll see you later." Layla couldn't stop smiling. She had one stop to make along the way. She needed to see Shane. Grabbing her purse from the hook by the door she called, "Lock up when you leave."

She hurried to her car, texting Shane along the way. Can I come over now? Need to talk to you.

At work, came his immediate response. Talk later? I'll come find you as soon as I get to Mia's birthday party.

Please, she texted back. It's important.

Layla arrived at Antoine's hotel an hour later. She wasn't surprised he'd opted to stay at one of the most opulent hotels in Boston instead of settling for more modest accommodations in New Suffolk.

She knocked on his door and waited for him to answer. A few minutes passed, and she knocked again.

The door opened and a bleary-eyed Antoine appeared. "Layla. What are you doing here?"

"I know we were supposed to meet for lunch, but I couldn't wait."

Antoine stepped back and gestured for her to enter

his suite. *"Mon amour."* He leaned in to kiss her and she stepped away.

"I can't come to Paris with you."

He gawked at her. "Why not?"

"I don't love you. I'm sorry."

"You don't love me?" Shock filled his gaze, but a moment later his expression cleared. "Darling." He grasped her hands in his and flashed a lazy smile. "Of course you do. I am the love of your life. You told me this."

He'd been her everything, until she'd found him in bed with another woman. He'd dismissed his indiscretion as if he'd done nothing wrong. "So much has changed since then. We don't belong together."

"Is this because of the man I saw you dancing with last evening?" Antoine's face filled with disdain.

"This is about the fact that I don't love you anymore. I'm sorry." Layla turned to leave.

"Wait." Antoine clamped his hand around her wrist and dragged her farther into the room. "Please sit." He pointed to the sofa in the living room. "I have something for you. You must see it." He rushed over to the desk that sat at the far end of the room, rifled through a bag and returned with a manila envelope a moment later. "I was going to save this for a wedding present, but you should have it now." His lips crooked into a winsome smile.

A wedding present? She pushed the envelope away. "We're not getting married."

"Open it, *s'il vous plaît.* I know you'll be pleased."

When she refused, he opened the envelope and handed her what looked like a legal document.

"I am giving you fifty percent ownership of Chez Antoine." His winsome smile turned into a smug grin.

Layla's mouth dropped open. She couldn't help it. "Why would you give me half ownership of your restaurant?" She scanned the paperwork, and yes, he was telling her the truth. It was all there in black and white. She and Antoine would be business partners. Like she'd wanted when they'd opened their place together.

"I need you, Layla." Antoine started pacing back and forth across the room. "The customers… They loved you, and they don't come anymore since you've been gone." He threw his hands up in the air. "Worst of all, the Michelin stars… They are gone, too."

Her fingers clenched into tight fists, crinkling the documents she held in her hands. "Let me get this straight. You want me back so that I can earn you the three Michelin stars back? All that stuff you said last night about missing me and how you can't live without me— It was so I'd come back to Paris and fix your restaurant?"

Antoine stopped in front of her and dropped down on one knee. *"Mon amour."* His smile made her nauseous.

She was never his love. She understood that now. He'd never been interested in her, only in what she could do for him. Thank goodness she'd found out what he was really like before it was too late.

Antoine chuckled. He aimed that slimy smile of his at her. "You had me worried for a moment, *ma chérie.*

So? Now you will come back to Paris with me and return to Chez Antoine."

Layla doubled over from a fit of laughter. The man had some nerve. "No."

Antoine looked a little taken aback. "Is it because of… What's his name?"

"Jealous, are we?"

"Not in the least." He straightened his shoulders and held his head high.

She looked Antoine dead in the eyes. "I won't allow you to use me ever again."

Antoine scoffed. "You complain about me, but that—" a look of distain crossed his face "—EMT of yours has done the same thing."

Layla sucked in a deep breath. "What are you talking about?"

"You think he helped you save your restaurant out of the goodness of his heart?"

She gawked at him. "How—did you know about that?"

"I am not stupid, Layla. I made sure I knew everything about your situation before I came back. Did he not tell you he'd lose his job if his precious fundraiser got canceled?"

Layla scrubbed her hands over her face. He'd told her the EMS department needed the funds the gala would generate. But he'd never made it clear how it would affect him personally.

"I guess the answer is no, judging by the look on your face." Antoine smirked. "So you see, your savior is no better than me."

He was messing with her head again. She shouldn't listen to him. He needed her to make Chez Antoine successful. Had always needed her to make his visions a reality.

But she… had already made her dreams come true. Happiness bubbled up inside her. "I don't need you. I never have." Layla ripped up the contract into tiny pieces and threw it up in the air. She watched Antoine's stunned expression as the pieces of paper fell to the plush carpet like confetti.

She flashed a mile-wide grin. "Goodbye, Antoine."

Layla held her head high as she marched out the door.

Shane exited the EMS building and strode through the parking lot to his truck. He needed to see Layla. Needed to tell her how much he loved her. Wasn't it just typical an emergency call came in immediately before his shift ended? He hoped it wasn't too late to say what he needed to say. What he should have said a while ago, if he were honest.

His phone buzzed. He glanced at the screen and read the text from his mother.

What's your ETA? Mia is already here. Her birthday party has started.

Damn. He hadn't realized how late it was. On my way now, he typed when he reached his truck. He'd talk to Layla before he joined the party.

Shane pulled into a parking space in the last row

at La Cabane de La Mer ten minutes later. The parking lot was full. Again. He grinned. How could Layla give all of this up?

Grabbing the present from the passenger seat, he hopped out and made his way to the entrance.

"Hi, Shane," the hostess called when he stepped inside.

"Hi." He couldn't remember her name.

"Are you here for the private party upstairs?"

"Yep."

"It's right this way."

The hostess pointed to the right, but Shane started toward the kitchen. "I'm going to speak to Layla before I head up."

He glanced into the dining room as he passed by. No empty tables could be found. She'd saved her restaurant, but at what cost?

"Layla's not here."

But she'd told him to meet her here. Said it was important. Had she changed her mind? Shane halted. He turned around. "Do you know where she is?"

The hostess shook her head. "No. Olivia said Layla asked her to cover for her last minute because something came up. I think it had something to do with that guy who came to see her last night during the EMS gala."

Layla was with Antoine? Bile burned in his gut. No, damn it. It couldn't be true. They hadn't talked yet. He hadn't told her how much he loved her.

"Hey, big brother." Piper walked out of the private dining room and into the waiting area. "I'm glad you finally arrived. The party is in full swing now." She rose on her tiptoes and planted a kiss on his cheek.

The last thing Shane wanted to do now was go to a party. "Sorry I'm late."

"No worries. Everyone understands you don't have a nine-to-five job. Sometimes things happen."

Did Layla understand, or had she left because he was late? No, damn it. Why was he assuming a worst-case scenario?

Love doesn't last. The snarky voice in his head wouldn't stop repeating the words.

Shane gave himself a mental shake. He needed to stop the madness.

"Come with me." Piper linked her arm through his. "Let me show you what I've done so far in setting up my gallery."

"Fine."

"You have to walk. I can't drag you. What's up with you?" Piper gave a lighthearted chuckle. "You're acting like one of the statues I'm planning on displaying in my gallery."

They walked into the private dining room. Just last night the room had been filled with tables topped with items for the silent auction. He expected those items to be gone now, but not the tables. "How come the room is empty?"

"Oh, we removed the tables this morning. Layla is letting me use this space as well for my gallery."

His stomach pitched and rolled. Layla wouldn't have given his sister the extra space if she was going to continue to run her restaurant. She'd need the space for customers, especially in the summer months.

"Hey, what's wrong with you?" Piper tugged on his arm. "You look like you're going to get sick."

He'd lost her. That's what she'd wanted to tell him this morning. His fingers started to shake. He needed to get out of here. Now.

"Piper, I found—"

Shane jerked his head toward the grand staircase. Layla stood on a step halfway down. His heart hammered in his chest. For a second, he wondered if his mind was playing tricks on him. He closed his eyes. When he opened them, Layla stood at the bottom of the stairs. "You're here." It was as if a sudden weight lifted from his chest.

Shane disengaged his sister's arm from his. He raced toward her.

"Hi." He swallowed hard.

"Hi." She stared at him.

He couldn't decipher the look in her eyes. *Hell.*

"You said you wanted to talk." His nerves jumped and jittered.

"I'll give you two some privacy." Piper passed by Layla as she headed up the stairs.

"I need to ask you a question." Her serious expression made his gut twist.

"Okay. What do you want to know?"

"Why did you help me save my restaurant?"

His brows furrowed. "I told you that first night. The EMS department needed the money from the gala and I wanted to ensure they received it.

"The town funding got cut and Mark thought he might have to let some of the staff go if they couldn't raise the funds needed. I assumed that since I was the last in, I'd be one of the first to go."

Layla bit her lip. "You didn't tell me that last part. About your job being in jeopardy."

"I didn't realize it had mattered to you. I'm sorry. I never meant to keep it a secret from you." He set the gift bag for Mia on the floor and grasped Layla's hands. Locking his gaze with hers, he said, "I wouldn't lie to you. I wouldn't betray your trust in that way. I know how much you were hurt when that happened to you before."

Shane thought he heard her mutter, "Win-win for both of us."

Layla nodded. "You've always leveled with me."

He shook his head. "No. I haven't." He looked away. He should have told her how he felt a long time ago. Squeezing their joined hands, he said, "And I need to make that right."

Her gaze filled with worry. "What are you talking about?"

Shane brushed his thumb back and forth across her cheek. He looked her in the eyes. "I'm in love with you, Layla Williams."

A slow smile crossed her lovely face.

"I can't say exactly when it happened. I've been trying like hell to deny the truth for a while now. I was scared. Of putting myself out there again. After everything I went through with my ex. But you…" He dropped a soft kiss on her parted lips. "You are worth the risk."

Her smile banished the darkness inside him.

"I love you, too." She leaped into his arms.

All the tension that had built up in him over the last twenty-four hours vanished with her saucy smile. He shook his head. "I should have marched into your office last night and told you how I felt." Instead, he'd let his fears rule him.

"I would have loved it if you had. Antoine—" Layla looked as if… Well, he wasn't quite sure what emotions were swirling inside her. She turned away from him. "Antoine didn't want me back. At least not the way you think. I was wrong about that."

"What do you mean?" Shane tugged her back into his arms once more. He lifted her chin and waited until she looked him in the eyes. "You can tell me. It's okay."

"Chez Antoine is suffering. His customers don't come since I've been gone. Even worse, he lost the three Michelin stars I earned. He offered me half ownership in his restaurant if I would come back."

Shane blinked. Had he heard her right? "He wants you as his business partner?"

"Yes," Layla confirmed. "That's what he proposed. Can you believe it?"

No. He couldn't. She'd have her French bistro. *Her dream.* Something she would *never* have if she stayed here, in New Suffolk. No matter how successful her restaurant became.

A tight band formed around his chest making it hard to breathe.

How could he take her dream away from her?

His stomach sank faster than a lead balloon. He couldn't. Wouldn't.

Shane straightened his shoulders and held his head high. He wasn't about to lose her now. He'd gotten a brief taste of what his life might be like without her and he didn't like it. "Go to Paris. Get your Michelin stars back. Make your dreams a reality. I'll go with you."

She gawked at him. "You can't do that. Your job…"

"It doesn't matter. I'll find something else to do. I'm going to Paris with you." He wouldn't take no for an answer.

"You love being an EMT."

"Not as much as I love you." It had taken almost losing her to realize what mattered most to him. Shane grinned and pulled her into his arms. "Sounds like you might need some help fixing things at this restaurant. I know a guy."

Layla shook her head and her serious expression returned. "You *can't* go to Paris."

His gut twisted. "Why not?" Had he misunderstood? No. Layla said she loved him.

"Because I'm staying here. In New Suffolk. With you." She placed a kiss on his lips.

"But your dream of owning your own French bistro…"

Layla grinned a mile-wide smile. "I have a new dream. I already have what I want right here. I was a fool not to realize that from the beginning. I should have told Antoine that from the start."

"What about your Michelin stars?" He tucked a stray lock of hair behind her ear. She'd worked hard to earn them and he couldn't take away the opportunity for her to get them back.

She smiled into his eyes. "I don't need them. Cooking good food that people love to eat is what matters to me. I have that here." She gestured around the restaurant. "How fortunate am I?" Her lips pressed against his again and lingered. "I have you, too." She deepened the kiss.

"Always." This time love would last. Of that he was one hundred percent sure.

Epilogue

One year later...

Layla stood in the empty dining room gazing out the large windows. She enjoyed the lull between the lunch and dinner rushes.

"Here you are, sweetie." Dad gave her a hug.

"We are so proud of you." Mom kissed her cheek.

"I knew you could do it." Zara threw her arms around her.

"I never had any doubt." Gramps appeared with Nonny by his side.

Layla arched a brow. "Not even when we almost lost this place?" She'd confessed everything to her grandparents, albeit after the restaurant was back in the black again.

"Even then," Grandpa confirmed.

"None of that matters anymore," Nonny added. "And you've paid the loan in full so there's nothing to worry about."

Layla grinned. The restaurant was doing well enough now that she'd been able to pay the loan off early. "As of this morning." She owned her place free and clear.

"Sorry I'm late." Shane rushed through the entrance. He walked over and gave Layla a quick kiss on her cheek.

"How is New Suffolk's newest paramedic?" Grandpa extended his hand to Shane.

Layla grinned. She was so proud of him. All his hard work had paid off.

"I'm well, sir. It's good to see you again." Turning to Layla, he said, "I'll be right back."

He disappeared into the kitchen and returned a few minutes later carrying a tray of glasses filled with champagne.

"Hey, don't start the party without us." Shane's mom walked in followed by his sisters and nieces.

Layla went over to greet them. "I'm so glad you could be here with us to celebrate."

"Are you kidding? We wouldn't miss this for the world." Piper kissed her cheek.

"We're so happy for you," Mia said.

"Us, too," Mia's girls added.

"Are we too late?" Elle rushed in and Abby followed.

"Nope. You're right on time." Shane held the tray out in front of him. "Everyone, take a glass. Sodas for you ladies," he added when his niece Brooke reached for a fluted glass. He set the tray down on the closest table and raised his glass. "To Layla. Congratulations on earning your fourth Michelin star."

She gave a gigantic smile. "The first for The Sea Shack."

Nonny shook her head. "If you were going to re-name your place, why couldn't you choose something... better?"

Gramps kissed Layla's cheek. "I think it's perfect."

She giggled. "Me, too. But Shane deserves the credit as much as I do." His love and support meant the world to her, and it allowed her to take her cooking to a whole new level.

Shane flashed a cocky grin. "Well, I did have to taste test all of your new creations before you put them on the menu."

"You like to cook." Piper pointed to Layla.

"And Shane likes to eat," his mother said.

"Now that's an understatement." Mia patted Shane's arm. "What?" she added when he pulled a face. "I'm just saying you guys make a great team."

"I agree." Shane walked over and stood in front of Layla. "We're perfect together. I can't think of any-one else I'd like to spend the rest of my life with." He dropped to one knee.

Layla gasped, and so did everyone else in the room.

"I love you, Layla. You're the best thing that's ever happened to me, and I've never been happier than I've been this past year with you. Will you marry me?"

Shane stood. He reached into his pocket and pulled out a ring box. He flipped open the lid. A round-cut solitaire diamond sat atop a diamond-studded white gold band.

"Yes." Layla threw her arms around him. "I can't think of anything I'd like better."

"Not even another Michelin star?" He flashed a cheeky grin.

Layla shook her head. "Not even ten Michelin stars." She didn't need them. "All I need is you. I love you, Shane Kavanaugh."

"I love you, too, and I can't wait to see what happens next on our journey."

She couldn't wait, either. But one thing was sure. They'd share a lifetime of love together.

* * * * *

Look for Piper Kavanaugh's story,
the next installment in
Sisterhood of Chocolate & Wine,
Anna James's new miniseries for
Harlequin Special Edition
Coming in 2024, wherever Harlequin books and
ebooks are sold!

HARLEQUIN
PLUS

Try the best multimedia
subscription service for romance
readers like you!

Read, Watch and Play.

Experience the easiest way to get
the romance content you crave.

Start your **FREE TRIAL** at
<u>www.harlequinplus.com/freetrial</u>.